Simply
Alice

Books by Phyllis Reynolds Naylor

King of the Playground
Shiloh
All but Alice
Josie's Troubles
The Grand Escape
Alice in April
The Face in the Bessledorf Funeral Parlor
Alice In-Between
The Fear Place
Alice the Brave
Being Danny's Dog
Ice
The Bomb in the Bessledorf Bus Depot
Alice in Lace
Shiloh Season
Ducks Disappearing
Outrageously Alice
The Healing of Texas Jake
I Can't Take You Anywhere
Saving Shiloh
The Treasure of Bessledorf Hill
Achingly Alice
Danny's Desert Rats
Sang Spell
Sweet Strawberries
Alice on the Outside
Walker's Crossing
Jade Green
Peril in the Bessledorf Parachute Factory
The Grooming of Alice
Carlotta's Kittens and the Club of Mysteries
Alice Alone

Simply
Alice

Phyllis Reynolds Naylor

Atheneum Books for Young Readers
NEW YORK · LONDON · TORONTO · SYDNEY · SINGAPORE

Atheneum Books for Young Readers
An imprint of Simon & Schuster Children's Publishing Division
1230 Avenue of the Americas
New York, New York 10020

Book design by Ann Sullivan
The text of this book is set in Berkeley Old Style.
Printed in the United States of America
First Edition
2 4 6 8 10 9 5 7 3 1
Library of Congress Cataloging-in-Publication Data
Naylor, Phyllis Reynolds.
Simply Alice / Phyllis Reynolds Naylor.—1st. ed.
p. cm.
Summary: In her freshman year, fourteen-year-old Alice experiences changes
and challenges with friends, family, and school activities, which leave her feeling
better about herself than ever before.
ISBN 0-689-82635-4
[1. Interpersonal relations—Fiction. 2. Brothers and sisters—Fiction. 3. High
schools—Fiction. 4. Schools—Fiction. 5. Theater—Fiction.] I. Title.
PZ7.N24 Si 2002
[Fic]—dc21 2001035539

To the one and only Claudia Mills

Contents

Simply
Alice

The Second Half

The thing about the second semester of ninth grade is you're not so scared anymore. You know how everything works—your locker, the cafeteria line, the buses, grading points—and you don't go to school every day with your heart in your mouth, expecting to be humiliated half out of your mind.

Which, of course, makes it all the worse when it happens. Wearing an ankle-length beige skirt with a long-sleeved cotton T-shirt, I was coming out of the cafeteria with my two best friends, Elizabeth Price and Pamela Jones, heading for P.E. on the ground floor. I'd had a hugely busy morning, starting with a meeting of the newspaper staff before school, and I still hadn't had a chance to duck into a rest room. After the big glass of orange juice I'd drunk for breakfast, and now the can of Sprite for lunch, I was in agony.

"Hey, guys, I've really, *really* got to go," I said as we started toward the stairs. I could only walk in tiny, mincing steps.

"We'll be in the locker room in three minutes," Elizabeth said.

"I can't wait three minutes," I told her, looking around as we approached the stairs. "I thought there was a rest room on this floor, maybe just beyond . . ."

What happened next was like a home movie on fast-forward. We must have been closer to the top step than I thought, because I was still looking around when suddenly I felt my body plunging forward, my books flying out in front of me.

I heard Elizabeth scream, "Oh, Alice!" and someone else shout, "Grab her!" and I could see the guys on the lower level look our way, but I was tumbling down the stairs, trying to grasp the railing as I went, and came to a stop on the second from the last step.

"Oh, my gosh!" Pamela yelled. "Are you hurt?"

I was pretty shaken, but within a few seconds I knew I wasn't hurt, not seriously—just bumps and bruises. My pride, mostly. I'd cut one knee, and my cheekbone stung. What I *was* conscious of was that my underwear and thighs were soaked, and it just kept coming. It was like someone had pulled a plug and I couldn't stop.

A tall senior had one hand under my back and another under my legs, and was lifting me to a standing position. "You okay?" he kept asking.

I wanted desperately for the earth to swallow me up, never to be seen again.

He must have felt the dampness because I saw him look behind me, like maybe I was broken and bleeding, and then he said gently, "My, my, my! That *did* scare the . . . uh . . . daylights out of you, didn't it?" He winked and walked away with the other guys, who didn't know what he was smiling about, and by that time Pamela and Elizabeth had reached the bottom of the stairs.

"Hide me," I choked.

"What? Are you all right? Are you hurt?" Elizabeth asked.

And then Pamela turned me around. "My gosh, Alice! You . . ." Trust Pamela to burst out laughing.

I backed up against the wall while kids stopped to pick up the pages of my three-ring notebook that were scattered all over the stairs. Then Pamela, walking ahead of me, and Elizabeth, walking behind, got me to the gym, and while the other girls played volleyball, I rinsed out my underwear and the back of my skirt, and held them under the blower to dry.

"Can anything be more humiliating than that?" I asked Elizabeth when we were showering later.

"You could have thrown up, too, while you were at it," she said.

At dinner that night, Dad said, "Al, what on earth happened to you?"

The left side of my face was bruised and swollen where I'd bumped against the stair rail. My real name is Alice Kathleen McKinley, but Dad and Lester, my twenty-two-year-old brother, call me Al.

"The most embarrassing thing that could possibly happen to a human being, that's all," I said, and launched into the whole dramatic story of how this handsome senior had knelt down to help me up and had felt my wet skirt. "Nothing in the world could be more awful than that," I repeated.

"Wrong," said Lester, passing the lentils and sausage, which, for anyone who cares to know, looks like mud. "He could have gathered you up in his arms, clutched your body to his, gazed into your eyes, and *then* you wet your pants."

"Well, believe it or not, there are some things in life worse than humiliation," said Dad. He, of course, means death and dying and wars and starvation, but it's sort of hard to think about those things when you're tumbling down a flight of stairs and losing control of your bladder at the same time.

I guess it's natural that my dad sees the serious

side of life, because my mom died when I was in kindergarten, and I suppose you never get over something like that. But now he's engaged to my seventh-grade English teacher, Miss Summers, and he's the happiest I've ever known him to be, even though she's on a teacher-exchange program in England.

"So other than using the school stairs as a toilet, how was your day?" Lester asked me.

"Well, a nice thing *did* happen," I said. "Since I'm one of the freshmen roving reporters for *The Edge,* and I'm also part of the stage crew for our spring musical, I'm supposed to write three articles on 'behind the scenes of a school production.' That should be fun."

"That's a great assignment," said Dad. "What musical?"

"Fiddler on the Roof."

"Oh, I like that one. Wonderful music!" Dad said.

"So what do *you* do, Al? Pull the curtain?" asked Les.

"All sorts of stuff," I told him. "Scene changes, props, costumes—wherever I'm needed."

"I'm glad to see you expand yourself a little. This may turn out to be a good year for you after all," said Dad.

What he means, of course, is that I may not go

to pieces or jump off a bridge or anything, just because Patrick and I broke up this last fall. Not that I would ever let somebody else make me so miserable that I'd do that. But it sure hadn't been an easy fall, watching Patrick and Penny, the "new girl in town," kissing around school and doing all the things together that Patrick and I used to do.

But I'm trying to pay more attention to other people and not be so self-centered. So I turned to Lester and said, "How was *your* day?"

"Interesting," he said. "I had coffee with one of my philosophy instructors."

"The babe?" I said, knowing that one of his teachers was really attractive, or so he'd told me. "I thought faculty weren't supposed to date students."

"Did I say 'date'? I said 'coffee,' Al. We talked. . . . Besides, she's not actually a professor, just an adjunct instructor. She'd *like* to be a regular member of the faculty, though, and she's got the brains to do it."

"You flirted, I'll bet," I said.

"That's not a felony. It's not even a misdemeanor."

"So . . . how old is she?" I wanted to know.

"A year or two older than I am, I suppose."

"Watch it, Les," I said, and grinned.

Dad was smiling, too. "Well, I had a letter from Sylvia today, and we're looking at July twenty-eighth to get married."

That was about the best news I'd had in two years. Two years of trying to connect the beautiful Sylvia Summers with my dad, and now they were really, truly, officially engaged, except that she didn't have a diamond or anything. Didn't even want one, Dad said.

"That's fabulous, Dad!" I said excitedly. "I hope she has ten bridesmaids and a symphony orchestra."

He laughed. "A simple little ceremony, Al, for family and friends. That's just the way we want it."

I guess, since it's their wedding, they can have whatever they want, but after working so hard to get them to fall in love, *I* thought we deserved an orchestra. A chamber quartet, anyway.

I was about as busy as I could imagine myself being, now that they were starting auditions for *Fiddler on the Roof*. The stage crew met three times a week after school, and it would become every day when we got closer to production. Actually the stage crew was divided up into lots of little crews, but most of us were on more than one—lighting, sound, sets, costumes, makeup, props, publicity. . . .

The real surprise was when Pamela told me she was dropping out of the drama club. I couldn't believe it. She's always talked about wanting to be an actress or a model, and she'd had the lead in our sixth-grade play.

"*Why?*" I asked, when she told me.

"I didn't know it was going to be a musical, and I don't think my voice is good enough for a leading role," she said.

"But you could be in the chorus, Pam! Or you could work behind the scenes. There's always something you could do."

"I don't want the chorus and I don't want to work behind the scenes. If I try out and don't make it, Mr. Ellis will remember that when I audition next year or the year after that. When I try out for the first time, I want to knock his socks off, and I can tell I'm not that good yet. I don't want a second-rate part. I want a major role."

I couldn't understand the feeling, never having wanted to be the center of attention that much.

"So I'm going to take voice lessons," Pamela finished. "Dad's already found a teacher for me and signed me up. But, listen! Elizabeth's got this great idea!"

We were on the bus going home, all squeezed together on one seat. Liz was by the window, I was in the middle, and Pam was on the end.

Pamela and Elizabeth were smiling. "Why don't the three of us sign up together as junior consultants for Tiddly Winks this spring!"

"Tiddly Winks?" I said in surprise. Tiddly Winks was an inexpensive earring store that had recently expanded to include accessories of all kinds—hair stuff, hats, scarves, belts, shawls, necklaces. . . . I tried to imagine myself a junior consultant. "What do you *do?*"

"It sounds really fun," Elizabeth assured me. "They're having a big promotion to advertise the new stuff in the store, and they want people to come in for a color and bone-structure analysis."

"*We're* supposed to do that?" I said. "What do I know about bone structure?"

"No, the professionals do that. Then they tell us what category the customer is in—like, she's a 'spring' or an 'autumn,' and 'angular' or 'round,' and then we show them all the colors and styles in her category."

"The thing is," Pamela continued, "we get points for every friend we bring in and points for every dollar each of our customers spends. When we get a certain number of points, we get free earrings or something."

"We're going to do it two evenings a week and on Sunday afternoons through the end of March," said Elizabeth. "We can all ride to the mall together."

I was beginning to feel squeezed in, and not just because I was sitting in the middle. "Hey, guys, I *can't!*" I said. "Between the Melody Inn on Saturdays and the newspaper and the stage crew, I'm stretched about as far as I can get already!"

"So give up the stage crew," said Pamela.

"*What?*"

"We joined the drama club together," she reminded me, "and now that I'm not going to try out, why don't you do Tiddly Winks with us? It's not as though you've got one of the major parts or anything. C'mon! Just tell them you don't want to do it, and sign up with Liz and me. We're going down tomorrow."

"I *can't!*" I croaked. "I already said I'd do it. I've been assigned to sets, props, and publicity."

"But that was when we thought we'd be going to rehearsals together," Pamela said. "Just tell them you changed your mind."

"But I *want* to do it!" I protested. "Just because you changed your mind doesn't mean *I* have to!"

Pamela seemed offended that I'd want to do something without her. "It's not as though you're the only one in school who can do the job, Alice. What's so important about being on the prop committee?" she asked.

"We could have so much fun together at Tiddly Winks!" Elizabeth said. "We'd have a blast. Of course, if you don't *want* to be with us . . ."

It did sound like it could be fun, but to tell the truth, the stage crew sounded better. I wasn't all that nuts about accessories. "I just can't," I said. "Don't be mad."

"Who's mad?" said Elizabeth, getting that look

on her face. "I just thought it was *something* the three of us could do together—you're always so busy on the newspaper."

"*You* guys can still do it!" I said. "I'll come down and you can do a color analysis on me."

"Whatever," said Pamela.

They'll get over it, I told myself. After all, Elizabeth hadn't joined the drama club when Pamela and I signed up, and we hadn't made a fuss about it.

For the first time, I was doing things on my own, and had made friends with another girl on the stage crew, a sophomore named Molly. She's shorter than I am, sort of squat, and wears overalls most of the time. Her hair is cut in a punk rock style, and she has the biggest, bluest eyes I've ever seen.

"So which of these things can you find?" Molly asked me the next day, after Mr. Ellis had distributed a list of all the different props we'd need.

"Not many," I said.

"Me either," said Molly. "It would help if one of us were Jewish, because all the characters in the musical are. Where are we going to find all this stuff?"

"We start asking, begging, pleading, borrowing, and hope we don't have to sell our bodies or resort to stealing," I joked.

There was one other girl who joined the stage crew, a junior. Her name was Faith, and she was tall, rail-thin, wore long, gauzy dresses of purple or black with beaded vests, black stockings, granny tie-up shoes with pointed toes, and lots of brace-lets. Her hair was long and very straight, and she wore pale, almost white, face powder with her lips and eyes outlined in black.

We liked Faith a lot, but we didn't especially care for her boyfriend, Ron Blake. He'd hang around at the back of the room when we had meetings, and never let Faith out of his sight. She even told him when she was going to the rest room. When it was just the two of them in the cafeteria or out on the school steps, they cuddled a lot, and Ron gave her tender kisses. But when she was around other people—I don't know; Ron seemed jealous or something.

He was there again on Thursday when we met after school, slouched in a chair off to one side, while Faith and Molly and I were checking things off our lists.

Pretty soon I heard Ron say, "Hey! C'mere!"

I don't think Faith heard him, because we were busy deciding who was going to try to get vests for the guys in the cast if they didn't come up with any themselves.

"Hey!" Ron said again, more loudly.

Faith glanced around and held up one hand, as if to signal, *Wait a minute,* and went on talking to us.

Ron got up from his chair and strode over to her. Faith looked up. *"What?"* she asked.

"Let's head out," he said, as though Molly and I weren't even there.

"I've got to finish here first," Faith answered.

He looked at his watch. "We leave here at four," he told her, and left the room.

Four wasn't time enough to do all we had to do, because we had each made a list of the props and clothes we were sure we could get, and those we still had to find. But this time when Ron came back he didn't call her name. He just walked up behind her, took hold of her long hair, and slowly tipped back her head until she was looking straight up at him.

"Owww!" she said, making a joke of it.

"Let's go," he said.

"Just a minute, Ron," she said, trying to work her hair free.

"Now!" he said.

Faith stood up, and he let go of her hair. "If you find any more of this stuff, call me, okay?" she said to us.

We nodded and Faith left, with Ron steering her by one shoulder.

Molly and I looked at each other. "I think maybe Faith has problems," I said.

"And he's number one," said Molly.

• • •

What helped make the breakup with Patrick bearable was that we were still speaking. In that first week or two after we split, I hid whenever I saw him coming, especially if he had Penny with him. Or I'd turn and go in a different direction. But that can get exhausting after a while, and I decided I just wasn't going to live that way anymore. So I started speaking to him and he to me, and when our whole gang got together, we acted like old friends. We *were* friends. In fact, Penny was part of our crowd now, and it got so that I didn't mind very much that she was around.

Except I could still remember Patrick's kisses and the way he touched me, and it still hurt to think of him giving those same kisses to Penny. There was also a sort of affectionate politeness between Patrick and me. Sometimes even a look that passed between us, as though we understood things nobody else could. But that was all. He was in an accelerated program to graduate one year early, so he was busy, I was busy, and it wasn't "Alice and Patrick" anymore, simply "Alice."

One day at lunch I was eating my chicken salad and talking to Elizabeth and Pamela when I suddenly stopped chewing and said to Pamela, "That girl looks *so* familiar." She looked like me from behind, actually—her body, anyway. Maybe that was why.

Pamela and Elizabeth turned and looked in the direction I was staring. A pretty girl was in line at the pizza counter. She was about my size, same color hair, and was wearing white cords and a gray top. Her thick hair was blow-dried back away from her face in wave after glorious wave. She was talking animatedly to a couple of boys who obviously were hanging on to her every word.

"She does!" said Elizabeth. "Who *is* she?"

Pamela stared intently at the girl, then back at me. And suddenly we both said it together: "Charlene Verona!"

"Is it?" said Elizabeth. "Are you sure?"

Charlene Verona was in sixth grade with us. She had everything going for her: looks, talent, boyfriends, grades. . . . Everything good seemed to happen to Charlene Verona.

"Tell you what," said Pamela. "I'll go up and say, 'We've missed you,' and if she says, 'I know, everyone has,' it's Charlene."

We laughed.

"No," I said. "I'll go up to her and say, 'How do you get your hair so shiny?' and if she says, 'Beauty runs in my family,' we'll know it's Charlene."

But neither one of us went up to the girl in the white cords because it was undoubtedly true: Charlene Verona was back, and if there were wonderful things waiting to happen to anyone at all in the next few years of high school, you could be sure they'd happen to Charlene.

Elizabeth, though, didn't remember her as well as we did. "What's the matter with her?" she asked. "I used to jump rope with her on the playground. I didn't think she was so bad. Why don't you like her?"

Pamela and I looked at each other again.

"She's perfect," said Pamela.

"And she knows it," I said.

"Oh," said Elizabeth, and shrugged.

But people can change, I told myself. I was all prepared to hate Penny for making a play for Patrick—and getting him—but I still had to admit she was funny, wasn't stuck on herself, or phony. . . . How did I know Charlene may not have changed?

"You know, Charlene might have changed a lot since we knew her," I said to Pamela as we left the cafeteria.

"I'm sure she has! For the worse," Pamela replied.

2

Cay ,

Elizabeth called me around the first of February.

"Where have you been?" she asked. "You weren't on the bus, and I've called you at least four times, but you weren't home yet."

"We had a staff meeting for the newspaper, and then Molly and I had to pick up a tablecloth a woman is loaning us for the Sabbath."

"The *Sabbath?*"

"The Sabbath supper in *Fiddler on the Roof.* We're trying to make the scenes as authentic as possible, and a woman said her grandmother brought a tablecloth over from Russia."

"Who's Molly?" Elizabeth asked, a whine in her voice. She's been going to a therapist to help her deal with her feelings about being molested when she was younger—by a family *friend,* no less—and lately she's been short-tempered. Hard to get along with sometimes.

"I've told you," I said. "I work with Molly and Faith getting props and things for the play. What's new with you?"

"Oh, nothing. The usual arguments with Mom. Why don't you come over after dinner?"

"I will," I said. "I thought you and Pamela were going to be down at Tiddly Winks for a while."

"That doesn't start till next week," she said.

It seemed I had less time for anyone anymore, myself included. When did I have a chance to cut my toenails? Write to Sylvia? Play cards with Dad? Go to a movie with Lester?

I walked across the street to Elizabeth's. She came to the door with Nathan in her arms. He's the one person who can always make Elizabeth smile these days. She'd been an only child until Nathan Paul was born about sixteen months ago, and now he's toddling all around the house and is into everything.

"I-yah!" he chortled when I came inside. That's what he calls me. I grabbed him from Elizabeth and swung him around, then blew on the side of his neck and he squealed happily, pulling away from me.

"He's a pill," Elizabeth declared. "Aren't you, Nate?" She kissed him.

Up in her room later, she was full of complaints. Her mom did this . . . her dad said that . . . no consideration . . . they never understood how she felt. I figured I didn't need to say anything, even if I'd known what to say, which I didn't. Maybe when you're seeing a therapist, all your angry feelings have to come out first before any positive ones can get through.

I was listening to what Elizabeth was saying, but what I was really looking at, or trying not to look at, was her chin, because right smack in the middle of it was a huge red pimple, and there was another on the left side of her forehead. She just had to feel awful about that—Elizabeth, who has always had skin like a china doll. I was lucky, I guess, because I usually got only a couple of pimples the week before my period, while Pamela had pimples on her forehead through most of middle school and still has some.

After a while I said, "Liz, you sound mad at the world. I hope you're not mad at me, too."

"Of course not," she said. "It's just, you're never around! At school you're always with kids we don't know."

"We eat lunch together, don't we?" I sighed sympathetically. "It's just the way things are going to be until the production is over. I promise I'll have you and Pam over soon."

"I'll believe it when it happens," Elizabeth said.

When I got home later and finished my homework, I checked my E-mail before I went to bed and found the usual messages from Karen and Jill and Pamela—one from Mark Stedmeister, even one from my old boyfriend, Donald Sheavers, back in Takoma Park. And then, near the bottom of the list, was an E-mail address I'd never heard of, and when I clicked "Read," it said:

> Have been watching you. Curious?
> Meet me at the statue outside the
> auditorium tomorrow morning, 8:10.

I could feel the blood throbbing in my temples. Who was *this*? Of course I wouldn't go. Was he nuts? Was it even a he?

Still, I *was* curious. I thought about all those "How We Met" letters to Ann Landers. What if this turned out to be Mr. Wonderful, and years from now I'd write some columnist and say that my future husband had once sent me an anonymous E-mail. . . .

I called Pamela.

"Oh, my gosh! That is major romantic!" she said. "Alice, you've just got to go!"

"I don't think so," I said. "What if he's a rapist or something?"

"Inside the school, main entrance, just before the first bell? Are you crazy?"

"Well, why didn't he sign his name?"

"He's just making an adventure out of it, that's

all. He's a romantic!" Pamela said. "Look, I'll even go with you. I'll stay back in the shadows and make sure you're all right."

"What if it's a grown man waiting there?"

"We'll report him to the office. Come on, Alice! It's probably someone you know."

"Well . . . okay. Just for the fun of it," I said.

She giggled. "Oh, Alice! What are you going to wear? Something sexy!"

"Pamela, you're out of your mind. I'm going to wear perfectly ordinary jeans and a sweater. And for Pete's sake, *promise* me you won't tell anybody. Not one word. I don't want an audience."

"Cross my heart," she said.

Of course, the first thing she did the next morning was tell Elizabeth, and Liz was hurt because I hadn't told her. But when she got over her snit, she said she wanted to come with us, too. So after we went to our lockers, we walked toward the auditorium.

"Okay, I've got it all figured out," Pamela said. "You know the kiosk at the top of the stairs? Elizabeth and I will hide behind that—actually, we'll just stand up there by the railing talking while you go down to the statue below, and we'll keep an eye on you. Make sure he isn't a serial killer."

I laughed. "This has got to be one of the stupidest things I've ever done."

"Huh-uh," said Liz. "Hiding Pamela up in your room last summer was the stupidest."

"No," said Pamela, "pulling my hair onstage in sixth grade was worse."

"Never mind," I said when we reached the kiosk. "Here I go."

Of course all three of us went to the stairs and looked down, but we didn't see anyone. The person could have been standing behind the statue, though.

"Good luck," said Elizabeth as I descended the steps in my best jeans, a white turtleneck, and my backpack. At the bottom, I thrust my hands in the pockets of my jeans and looked around. Kids were coming through the doors from the buses, swarming around the statue, heading for their lockers. No one seemed to be lingering.

"Hey, Alice, you're going the wrong way," someone called as she passed. I went over to one side and leaned back, one foot against the wall behind me, real casual, real cool. I felt that whoever the person was was watching me, but as the minutes ticked by and a couple kids looked at me as they passed, I could feel my face beginning to color. I glanced at my watch: 8:14. The note had definitely said 8:10. The bell would ring at 8:20.

I decided to give it one more minute. Out of the corner of my eye, I could see Pamela and Elizabeth looking over the railing in the hall above, wondering the same thing I was: *Where the heck was he?*

At 8:15, I pushed away from the wall and quickly went back up the stairs. I knew my face was bright red, and wished like anything I'd never told Pamela, that I had suffered through this alone.

"Let's go," I murmured, taking big strides back down the hall.

"I wonder why he never showed," Elizabeth said, hurrying to catch up with me.

"I don't know, but whoever wrote the note I don't even *want* to meet. He was probably somewhere watching, laughing his head off."

At the corner I stopped. "Listen, if you two are my best friends, you will never, ever, tell anyone else about this."

"Oh, we wouldn't!" said Elizabeth.

"Not a soul," said Pamela.

I checked my E-mail when I got home that day. Nothing. But when I checked it again just before going to bed, I found this:

> *I'm really sorry about this morning if you were at the statue. Our bus had to go around the construction on Dale Drive and we were late. Would you give me one more chance? Meet me at the statue today at 12:35?*
> *CAY (Crazy About You)*

I clicked "Delete" and turned my computer off.

On Saturdays at the Melody Inn, I run the Gift Shoppe. It's under the stairs leading to the second floor, where instructors give music lessons in soundproof cubicles. Dad's the manager of the store, and Marilyn Rawley, one of Lester's former girlfriends, is assistant manager.

We sell all kinds of stuff in the Gift Shoppe—from novelty items to useful things like guitar picks, batons, mouthpieces, and strings. Dad usually handles the instrument sales, Marilyn the sheet music, and I do the Gift Shoppe. There are other part-time clerks who help out on evenings and weekends.

In January, we have a big sale to get rid of the stuff we overstocked for Christmas, and make room for new things. Salesmen come by with catalogs of new music boxes in the shape of violins, sweatshirts with keyboards on both sleeves, men's shorts with clef signs, scarves with the *Moonlight Sonata* printed on them, earrings in the shape of middle C, and all sorts of jewelry for the revolving glass case beside the counter.

"Hi, how you doing?" Marilyn said when I came in on Saturday. Her brown hair is straight and shoulder length, curled under at the ends, and she wears a lot of Indian prints. Today she had on a calf-length black wool skirt with a slit up the side, and a green silk blouse with embroidery on both sleeves. I always wished she and Les would get back together. I think Marilyn would in the blink of an eye, but I don't know about Lester.

"Busy," I told her. "That's the one word that describes high school—busy, hectic, tense. . . ."

"How about 'exciting, different, challenging'?" Marilyn said.

"Well, that, too," I told her.

She gave me a computer printout listing all the merchandise we had ordered for the Gift Shoppe within the last year.

"We'll be doing inventory next week," she said. "What we need you to do is cross out any item that we've sold out completely."

I set to work on the printout sheet and was halfway through when I heard someone say, "Excuse me, but there's no one in sheet music. Could you help me?"

I turned around to see Charlene Verona, The Girl Who Has Everything.

"Hey . . . aren't you . . . Alice McKinley?" she said. "Weren't we in sixth grade together?"

"Yes," I said. "You're Charlene, aren't you?"

"Yes! Oh, it's great seeing all my old friends! We just moved back here the first of the year, and it's like I never left!"

What I wanted to say was, *Whoop-dee-do*. What

I said was, "What do you need from sheet music?"

But she went bubbling on: "Dad was transferred to Illinois and I just *hated* it there. I mean, I had to start all over again and I didn't know anyone, but now we're back and he promises I can complete high school in Silver Spring, so here I am!"

"Here you are!" I repeated. "What can I get you?" *Why did I dislike her so much?* I wondered.

"I'm trying out for *Fiddler on the Roof* and I need to learn some songs. Do you have a songbook from the musical?"

"I think so," I said. I used my key to lock the cash register, then went over to sheet music. Both Dad and Marilyn were helping students in the instruments section, and the part-time clerk was on a rest break.

"I just love that musical," Charlene said as she followed me across the store. "I want to play Tevye's daughter Hodel. She sings that gorgeous song about wherever her lover is, that's home. Do you know it?"

I didn't, exactly, but I secretly hoped we were out of the music. At the same time, I made a mental note that we should order more songbooks immediately, because other kids were going to be coming in looking for them.

I went to the file cabinet marked MUSICALS and began looking through file folders in alphabetical order. There it was, only one copy left—the songbook for *Fiddler on the Roof.*

My first thought was to tell her it was already sold, then buy it myself, give it to Pamela, and urge her to learn the songs and try out. But then my mature self took over, and I knew that was Pamela's decision to make, not mine.

"Here you are," I said, and rang up the sale.

"How about you?" Charlene asked. "Aren't you going to try out?" And then her face froze and she said, "Oh, I'm sorry, Alice. I forgot you can't sing. Me and my big mouth."

She didn't have to put it that way. Of course I can sing. I just can't carry a tune, that's all. It's embarrassing enough without having to be the daughter of a man who manages a music store.

"Eighteen dollars and ninety cents," I told her.

She kept trying to make it up to me. "Oh, well. You must be horribly busy here. I'll bet it's fun to work in a music store."

"Out of twenty," I said stonily, taking the bill she handed me, and gave her the change.

"Thanks, Alice!" she said. "See you around school! Wish me luck!" And she was off.

"In a pig's eye," I muttered.

Marilyn came hurrying over. "Thanks. We're a little shorthanded this morning. Did the girl get what she needed?"

"No," I said. "What she needed was a punch in the mouth, but she got *Fiddler on the Roof* instead.

By the way, we need to rush order lots more of those songbooks."

Marilyn gave me a quizzical smile. "Friend?"

"The Girl We Love to Hate," I said. "The girl who gets everything she sets her heart on."

Marilyn studied Charlene as she left the store, and then me. "Nobody gets *every*thing they want, Alice. Trust me," she said, and I knew she was referring to Lester.

I told her then about the E-mail message from someone signing himself CAY. How I'd gone to the statue but no one was there, and about the follow-up apology.

"I sure wouldn't take it any further if I were you," Marilyn said. "Any guy who can't introduce himself isn't the kind you want to get involved with."

"That's about what I figured," I told her. What I didn't tell her, though, was how I kept looking at all the guys in my classes, wondering, *Was it him? Was it him?*

3

Heart of Gold

I don't wear a lot of jewelry—I like a simple look—but for my birthday last year, Aunt Sally in Chicago, Mom's older sister, gave me a small gold heart-shaped locket that used to belong to my mother, with a lock of Mom's hair in it. It was the same color as mine, strawberry blond.

I'm not sure how Aunt Sally came to have it in the first place—maybe Mom left all her jewelry to her sister when she died—but Aunt Sally felt I should have it. And maybe she'd saved it for my fourteenth birthday because she felt I'd be responsible enough by then to take good care of it.

In eighth grade I wore it a couple of times, but when I put it on over a navy blue sweater in ninth, I liked the look so much that I began to wear it often.

"It's nice, Alice," Elizabeth said once. "Who gave it to you?"

"It's something of Mom's," I answered.

That's one thing that bothers my dad, that I don't talk about Mom more. I don't think he realizes how little I remember of her. I was only five or so when she died, and they say kids don't remember much before the age of four. Combine this with the fact that Aunt Sally took care of us for a few years after Mom's death, so a lot of my memories are confused with Aunt Sally.

"Did you hear any more from Cay?" Pamela asked me at school one day. We started calling him—or her—Cay, because we didn't know how else to refer to him.

"Maybe he's a member of the faculty and he can't reveal himself," said Elizabeth. "Maybe all he can do is worship you from afar, Alice, and the day you graduate from high school, he'll profess his undying love, and you'll find out he was your algebra teacher or something."

"Maybe he's the custodian," said Pamela, grinning.

"Or the bus driver," said Elizabeth.

"The principal!" said Pamela.

"I'm not interested," I told them. "Somebody was obviously playing a joke to see if I'd fall for it."

Between fifth and sixth periods, I literally bumped into Patrick in the corridor, and we walked as far as my history class.

"How's it going?" he asked.

"Busy," I answered. "Exams in all my classes, inventory at the store, stage crew for *Fiddler on the Roof* . . . How about you?"

"I may graduate in three years, but they'll probably have to carry me across the stage," he said. "This semester's a lot worse than last."

"I'll bet!" I said. "Patrick, you always were a brain."

He just grinned. "See you," he said.

I'll admit I felt sort of down on Valentine's Day. What I tried not to think about was what Patrick was giving Penny as a present—that he was kissing her, stroking her hair. I wore my heart locket to school—sort of a talisman, I guess, against hurt. I couldn't help studying Penny in the cafeteria at lunchtime, trying to see if she was wearing anything Patrick might have given her. To her credit, she didn't mention either him or Valentine's Day. She could have rubbed my face in it, but she's not that kind of girl. I don't think Patrick would have fallen for her if she was.

I found myself listening for Penny's name over the speaker system, though. In our high school, I discovered, guys sometimes send flowers to their girls in care of the school office. Some of the teachers' husbands do it, too. Then the school secretary calls out those persons' names between classes, and they go down to the office and collect their bouquets.

My face felt hot just thinking about it. It was such a public declaration of love—wonderful if it happened to you, horrible if it happened to someone you envied. If Penny went around all day carrying flowers from Patrick, how could I stand it? But only a dozen or so girls got their names called, and we—The Forgotten Others—tried not to look daggers at them.

Faith, though, got a bouquet from Ron—*roses, no less*—and you just had to be glad for her. You'd think it was the most wonderful moment of her life, the way she brightened, and I figured Ron couldn't be all bad if he could make Faith that happy.

Penny's name was never called. At least, I didn't hear it if it was.

Maybe I was feeling especially low because not only did I not have a boyfriend, but I had the vague feeling that Elizabeth and Pamela and I weren't as close as we were at the beginning of ninth grade. They've been my two best friends since seventh, and I think they're still best friends with each other. Just not with me.

It's so subtle, though. Nothing I can put my finger on. I wouldn't even know how to bring it up. When I say, "Are you mad?" Liz says, "Of course not!" But they don't call me like they used to, and I think—I *know*—they do things together on weekends without even asking if I want to come. Of course I don't call them as often, either, but they know how busy I am right now. And they've been having a ball at Tiddly Winks. On the bus to school they're always showing the other girls what earrings they've got so far for being junior consultants.

Did I just imagine it, I wondered, or did Pamela show the pair of turquoise teardrops to everyone on the bus but me? Was I being oversensitive to the fact that Elizabeth invited four girls to come to Tiddly Winks on Friday night—promised they'd all go out for pizza afterward—and then, suddenly looking in my direction, seemed to invite me as an afterthought?

When they did talk to me, it sounded too polite, too forced—not the chummy, teasing way we used to be with each other. But how exactly do you accuse someone of being too polite? Too cold? I kept waiting for an opening—for something bigger to happen, so I could say, "What's wrong?" But I already knew. We were starting to grow away from one another, to look around at other friends, which is what you're supposed to do as you grow up, I guess, but all it made me want to do was cry. I'd thought we were going to be best friends forever.

• • •

Dad confided at dinner that he had sent a dozen roses to Sylvia Summers in Chester. Even my brother looked amazed.

"Well, *that* must have set you back big bucks!" he said.

"I won't even tell you how much," Dad said. "It was just something I wanted to do."

I stared at him over the spaghetti. Dad looked like a fuzzy teddy bear in his plaid flannel shirt and Docker pants—his scruffies, he calls them—the most comfortable clothes he can think of when he gets home from work. "You had a dozen roses flown to England?" I exclaimed.

Dad laughed. "No, hon. I called a florist here who takes international orders. He calls a florist in Chester, and that florist delivers the flowers."

Sylvia called Dad about seven. She'd found the roses when she got home from school, she told him, and even though it was midnight there, she and Dad were on the phone for a long time.

I spent the last hour before bed E-mailing some of my friends. Even though I doubted they'd answer, I told Pamela and Elizabeth about Dad sending roses to Sylvia, checked with Karen about the history assignment, and tried to find out from Jill if she'd gone to the Valentine Dance. What I really wanted to know was whether Penny and Patrick had been

there, and they had. Just before I signed off, the red
flag on my "You've Got Mail!" box went up, so I
checked the incoming mail once more and found
this message:

> Still watching, still admiring. Would
> you give me another chance?
> CAY

This time I E-mailed back:

> If you really want to meet me, you'll
> walk up and say Hi.

There was something creepy about this, but I
sure wasn't going to tell Elizabeth or Pamela about
it this time.

When I got home from the Melody Inn on Saturday,
there was a message on the answering machine.

"Where *were* you?" came Elizabeth's voice, sharp
and brittle-sounding. "You could at least have let
me know if you couldn't make it!"

I immediately dialed her number. "Liz? What are
you talking about? Where was I *when?*"

"Last night! At Tiddly Winks. You said you'd
come, and I'd invited four other girls for pizza
afterward. We didn't know whether to wait for you
or what."

"Oh, my gosh!" I said. "We had a meeting after

school, and it dragged on, and when I got home I just heated leftovers for my dinner and stretched out on the couch. I completely forgot!"

"If we bring in five girls at once, we get bonus points and Tiddly Winks pays for the pizza afterward. Because I only had four girls, I lost the bonus points and had to pay for their dinner myself. If I'd known you weren't coming, I could have invited someone else."

"I'm really sorry! I guess I just conked out. Listen, I'll pay for the pizza, Liz."

"Oh, never mind," she said.

"No! Really!"

"Forget it," she said.

Mr. Ellis was holding tryouts for *Fiddler on the Roof,* and the big buzz was that Charlene Verona would get the part of Hodel. Every day after school the first two rows of the auditorium were filled with hopefuls, who were called up onstage one at a time and asked to sing a song from *Fiddler.* Any piece they wanted. Charlene did well with "Far from the Home I Love."

The stage crew attended just to be part of the general excitement. Each actor would be required to furnish his or her own costume, but we were supposed to help out and find anything that an actor couldn't. I'll admit, I wished I could sing. I wished I had the nerve to be up there all by myself, with Mr. Ellis and the others looking up at me, while I belted out a song un-self-consciously to the piano accompaniment.

Dad said that my mother used to sing—that she was tall, that she liked to wear slacks a lot, was a good swimmer, and always made him a pine-apple upside-down cake on his birthday. And they loved each other a lot. Maybe Dad, being musical, loved her *especially* because she could sing. I wondered what went wrong in me.

I was sitting in the next to the last row in the auditorium with Faith and Molly when Charlene's turn came to audition a second time. The kids who were most likely to get a part were called back again; the others were thanked and told they could leave. If you didn't get a callback, you were either out, or were part of the chorus. This time Mr. Ellis had several girls go onstage together, singing different songs, saying the speaking parts, listening to the sounds of their voices and how they looked and sounded together.

"Charlene really wants to play Hodel," said Faith, propping one delicately booted foot on the back of the seat in front of her. "I heard she'd kill for the part."

"I don't know," I said. "That small girl in the tan shirt has a great voice, too."

"Mr. Ellis has to look at all the parts—who's going to play Golde, who's going to play the other two sisters—all of that," Molly told us. "I think Kurt Weinstein is going to get the part of Tevye. He's got a terrific voice."

He did, too, After Charlene sang a second time, Kurt went up onstage. He's a senior, a big guy—goes out for wrestling as well as choir—and as soon as we heard him, we knew he'd get the part. He not only sang, he gestured and strutted around the stage, and we clapped like crazy when he'd finished.

"Hey!" came a whisper, and I turned to see Ron Blake in the row behind us. He reached forward and stroked Faith's cheek and she responded by kissing his fingers.

Down in front, though, Mr. Ellis was asking another guy, who was also auditioning for Tevye, to come up and sing. He wanted to compare the two, and so did we. It was sort of hard to concentrate with all the cheek-stroking and finger-kissing going on beside me, but Ron, I guess, can only be kind for so long. I think he resents Faith doing anything that doesn't involve him.

"Hey, babe, let's go," he whispered.

"I want to stay long enough to hear this guy sing. See if he's as good as Kurt," Faith whispered back.

Ron especially doesn't like Faith paying attention to other guys, even to the way they sing.

"Well, I want to leave now," he told her.

It was all I could do to keep from saying, *Well, she doesn't, so get your big self out of here,* but I didn't.

Faith turned around again, facing the stage, and Molly and I sort of leaned toward her, helping pin her in to strengthen her resolve. The second guy went up onstage and sang "If I Were a Rich Man." Suddenly a big foot appeared beside my face, and I turned to see that Ron had stuck both his feet up on Faith's shoulders and was holding her head in a vice grip with his heavy boots.

She just gave a little laugh and went on watching the stage. When she didn't react, he clamped his boots tighter against her face and began rocking her head from side to side. Both Molly and I turned around and glared at him.

"Leave her alone," I said.

His eyes narrowed, and he studied me for a long moment as though he had designs on me, too. I'd seen him look at me like that before. Was he "the watcher," I wondered? Could he be CAY?

"Who asked your opinion?" he said.

"Nobody. You got it for free," I said.

"Oh, Alice!" Faith whispered.

"Quit being such a bully!" put in Molly.

Ron put his feet down and leaned forward,

grabbing Faith's shoulder. "We're leaving," he said.

And to our dismay, Faith got up. "I've gotta go," she said, maneuvering past Molly's legs, and left the auditorium with Ron.

Molly slid over beside me. "He is really bad news," she whispered.

"I know. What does she see in him?"

"He gives her a lot of attention, all the wrong kind," Molly said.

Kurt got the lead. The names were posted on the bulletin board beside the orchestra room on Friday. Most of the cast were juniors and seniors, and Charlene lost out on Hodel but got the part of Tzeitel, the oldest daughter—a huge plus, considering she's only a freshman. But the other two girls chosen for daughters were smaller in size than Charlene and their voices were higher, even though they were seniors, so Mr. Ellis knew what he was doing, I guess. I decided that even if Pamela had tried out, she wouldn't have gotten a part, so maybe she was right to wait for her junior or senior year.

But there was no time to talk with her about it. I was going to E-mail her, but forgot, and when I finally sat down at the computer, I found there were two old E-mails from her I'd never answered. The fact was, I often had to go to school early for a meeting of the newspaper staff, and I stayed every day after school to work with the stage crew, and only rode the bus a few times a week.

When I got on one morning, Pam and Liz were laughing together at some private joke. I took the seat behind them, got up my nerve, and finally leaned over the back of their seat, trying to sound as friendly as I could. "What's up?" I asked.

"Nothing. What's with you?" said Elizabeth.

"Everything's going on at once," I said. "I feel I'm going around in circles."

"So we've noticed," said Pamela.

"You guys want to get together this weekend?" I asked. "Saturday night, maybe?"

"Busy," said Pamela.

"Sunday?"

"We've got Tiddly Winks then," said Elizabeth.

"Sunday night?" I offered.

"Sorry," said Elizabeth. "I've got something going on."

"Gosh, I'm not the only one who's crazy busy right now," I told them.

"Yeah," said Pamela, and turned to look out the window.

At lunchtime, when I got my tray in the cafeteria, I was heading to the table where I always sit when Molly, at a closer table, waved me over. I looked across at where the gang had gathered, and the only vacant spot was beside Pamela, across from Elizabeth. If the noontime conversation was going to be anything like it had been on the bus that morning, why put myself through it?

"What's up?" I said, sliding in beside Molly. And we chatted about the musical.

"What did you think of the casting?" she asked me, vigorously attacking her ham and cheese sandwich.

"Ecstatic that Kurt got the lead. He's perfect!" I said. "The choice for Golde was good, too."

"Tzeitel was a surprise, though. Charlene Verona's the only freshman who got a part. Her voice is great, but a lot of girls in the chorus are jealous," Molly said.

She went back and got two ice-cream cups for us, and I was just finishing mine when Pamela and Elizabeth and Brian Brewster walked by, taking their trays to the counter.

"Hey, Al!" said Brian. "What's the matter? We're not good enough for you?"

I could tell he was joking, and I quickly tried to make a joke of it myself. "No, I'm just too popular, I guess," I said laughing.

I saw Elizabeth and Pamela nudge each other as they walked on by. I put my head in my hands. Why did I say *that*? Why is it that sometimes your mouth says the very worst thing possible, like it's detached from your brain? I didn't want to live like this, having to be so careful! It was like walking on eggshells. I had to watch every single thing I did or said or somebody got mad.

"Headache?" Molly asked.

"Big time," I told her.

I decided I just couldn't afford to get upset right then. There was too much to do, and I had to turn in the first of my articles to the school paper, not to mention homework which was piling up like mad. My first article would be about tryouts—the hopefuls, the feeling of being left out and stuff. I wouldn't use any names, of course. But I wanted to get inside the skin of every person who gets up onstage and sings, knowing afterward that you haven't done your best, that others were better than you, that the director's comments about your "nice" voice were just that, "nice," but not too exciting. And yet, it couldn't be a put-down of the kids who had ended up in chorus. I couldn't make them sound any less important.

So I wrote the piece from my own viewpoint— a girl who couldn't carry a tune, so she was content to work behind the scenes painting sets and gathering props and leaving the glory to others. I wrote it humorously, and was really surprised when Sara and Nick, the editors, put it on the third page of our four-page newspaper. First page is best, of course, but third is next best, because your eye falls on the third page when you open the paper.

I started out: *For a girl who can't carry a tune, being a member of the stage crew for the spring musical,* Fiddler on the Roof, *is as close as I'll ever get to glory. . . . And I ended with: . . . so here I stand, paintbrush in hand, while those braver than I, and certainly more talented, sing their hearts out up onstage, knowing that while only a few of them get the coveted roles, the rest of us will provide the backup, the greasepaint, and the props to get this production off the ground.*

I was amazed at the response. Kids came up to me the next day and said, "Loved the article, Alice." And, "You really can't carry a tune?" Stuff like that. Patrick stopped me as I was coming out of gym and put one hand on my shoulder. "Enjoyed the article, Alice. Really funny."

Mr. Ellis liked it a lot. So did Faith and Molly.

"You said it for all of us," said Faith. "Except I really wouldn't want to be up there onstage. I like behind-the-scenes stuff."

"Really?"

"Yeah. You know what I'd like to do? Work for some repertoire company. Be one of the permanent stage crew that dresses all in black and comes onstage to change props between scenes."

"Maybe you will," I said. "Where would you go? New York?"

"Yeah, that would be best, but I'll probably end up going wherever Ron does," she said.

The two people who didn't mention the article at all were Elizabeth and Pamela. When I got on the bus that afternoon, they were so busy talking about Tiddly Winks that they had everyone's attention and ignored me completely. I asked them a question and they answered, but then they went right on talking, their voices unnaturally high and loud, and I knew they were putting on a show just to hurt me. I could hardly stand it. How could girls who liked each other as much as we did suddenly turn on one of their own this way? Couldn't they see that I was drowning in work right now, but it wouldn't always be this way?

I decided that when Elizabeth and I got off the bus together, I would confront her about it. But when we reached our stop and I stood to get off, Liz stayed where she was and I knew she was going on to Pamela's. I walked home alone, tears in my eyes.

Why does everything have to stay exactly as it is or somebody gets mad? I knew they resented Molly and Faith, but wasn't I allowed to have other friends? Did it have to be just "Alice, Elizabeth, and Pamela" forever? I wondered how I'd feel if Elizabeth joined a club I didn't belong to, and seemed to be spending all her time there. Or if Pamela got a new friend and did things with her that she didn't do with me. I probably wouldn't like it, either, but once *Fiddler on the Roof* was over, we could be closer again. I just had to ride it out, I decided.

I was still getting compliments about the article on Monday, and could feel my face flush with excitement when anyone praised my writing. Several teachers commented on it, too. I ducked in the rest room once to see if my face looked as warm as it felt, and suddenly my heart seemed to be beating double time because the gold locket I'd put on that morning was gone. There was my face and the white expanse of my sweater beneath it, but no gold locket, not even the chain.

I panicked. My mother's gold locket! The only real piece of my mother I had left—her hair. I retraced my steps as fast as possible, all the way back to my last class, but couldn't find it. I checked my pockets, my backpack. Then, crying, I went to the school office to ask at Lost and Found.

"We'll let your homeroom teacher know if it's turned in," the school secretary said. I had to get a pass to my next class and went in, my eyes red.

There was a stage crew meeting again after school, so I was late going home. But when I got to my locker for my jacket, I found a piece of paper stuck in one of the narrow ventilation slots.

> I think you dropped your locket leaving class today. I tried to slip it through this slot, but the heart was too big to go through. If you'll meet me at the statue at 8:10 tomorrow, I promise I'll be there and will give it to you then.
>
> Crazy About You

4

Behind the Curtain

I wanted my locket back.

Could CAY—the watcher, the stalker—possibly have unfastened it somehow? But even as I thought it, I remembered having trouble with the hook that morning when I put the locket on. Maybe it hadn't been fastened completely. The note said I'd dropped it when "leaving class today." Did that mean this person was in a class with me? Which one?

I didn't tell anyone about CAY this time. I couldn't have told Pamela or Elizabeth if I'd wanted to, because they didn't answer my E-mails anymore. We said "hi" to each other in the halls, out of courtesy, but then they turned away or I turned away. As I sat staring out the bus window the next morning, I wondered again how this could have happened to us in the space of a few weeks.

Deep inside, I knew that what I should do was go over to Elizabeth's house, invite myself in, and have a face-to-face talk with her. Apologize for anything I'd done wrong. But I was angry, too. I *hadn't* done anything except get involved in school activities that didn't include them. Make friends with girls they didn't know. Was this the way it had to be when you were best friends with someone— they controlled your life, who you could see, what you could do? Is that what was happening with Faith and Ron?

They're the ones who should apologize, I told myself, and so I just stared out the window and thought angry thoughts while Pamela and Elizabeth, sitting behind me, were probably doing the same—all three of us making ourselves miserable.

At school, I got off first and headed for the corridor where my locker was, but when I was sure they had gone to theirs, I backtracked and went down the stairs to the auditorium. Once again, no one was there—just kids coming from their buses, heading for class. If he stood me up again . . . !

I glanced at my watch. Nine minutes after eight. I turned slowly around, studying every person coming toward me, but they all went by. When I turned again, I was face-to-face with a familiar blond guy several inches taller than me, wearing an Eddie Bauer jacket, a backpack over one shoulder.

He just smiled and held out an envelope. I took it. I could feel the shape of the locket inside.

"Thanks," I said. "I don't know where I dropped it."

He was in my biology class, and had thick blond eyebrows that formed a bridge over his nose, a mouth that turned slightly down at the corners when he smiled. He opened his mouth then, but nothing came out. Instead, he blinked his eyes a couple of times and finally he said, "O-O-On the floor in b-b-b-biology."

I kept looking at him. "Are you Cay?" I asked, then felt myself blush when I realized he wouldn't know I'd been referring to him by those initials. It was his turn to stare now, and then he got it. He grinned and nodded.

For some reason, we both laughed.

"You sit over by the window, don't you? Second table?" I asked.

"Yeah."

"I was afraid you were a stalker. Some creep who was going to follow me around school the rest of the year."

He laughed again. "N-Not to worry."

I looked at my watch again. "I've got English first period."

"Me, t-too," he said. "Mr. Larson."

"Worrell," I told him, and we started walking

together. I glanced over at him. "Do you always E-mail girls you want to meet?"

This time he didn't look at me, just smiled, his eyes straight ahead. "Just you."

I smiled back. "I don't bite."

He laughed then, and changed the subject. "That was a g-great ppp-piece in *The Edge*."

"Thanks," I said. "It was a lot of fun to write." We'd reached my class. "Thanks again for returning my locket. It was Mom's and it's all I really have of her. A lock of her hair, I mean."

He looked serious then. "She died?"

"Yeah. When I was five. My aunt gave me this locket of Mom's for my fourteenth birthday."

"I'm really sss-sorry," he said.

"But Dad's getting married again this summer. To my seventh-grade English teacher. It's really wild." I glanced inside the classroom. "Anyway, thanks . . . uh . . . Eric?"

"Yeah. Eric F-Fielding."

"I'll see you," I said.

"See you," he answered, and walked away. Smiling.

When I sat down in my chair, I opened the envelope. There was Mom's locket, and inside, the lock of her hair. No note. Just the locket, as he'd said.

I slipped it around my neck and made sure it

was fastened right this time. He seemed nice. Sort of shy, maybe. Possibly because he stuttered. But at least I knew he wasn't some creep. Wait till I told Pamela! And then I remembered about Pamela and Elizabeth, and felt hollow inside.

This wasn't right! I told myself. I shouldn't have to feel guilty about making new friends. The problem was that Elizabeth was too wrapped up right now in her own troubles to take on anything else, and Pamela, who had always seemed self-confident to me, had gotten scared off by the competition in high school and wanted to return to the safe little threesome we used to be. In a way, I wanted that, too, but I also wanted more.

I told Dad and Lester about Eric at dinner that night. Before dinner, actually. Dad was cooking Chinese, and when he does that, Les and I have to get all the veggies chopped and ready to throw into the wok when he wants them.

"He seems really nice, just shy," I said. "And he stutters."

"You've got to watch out for shy, stuttering guys," said Les, dropping a handful of bean sprouts into the wok as Dad stirred them around in the oil.

"Why?"

"They'll grab a girl's heart every time because they seem so vulnerable."

"Oh, I don't know. Eric looks as though he could take care of himself very well," I said. "Were you ever shy?"

"Was I ever *shy?* Why, I'd flatten myself up against a wall so tight you'd think I was wallpaper," Lester said. "If a girl came up to me at a school dance, I'd be looking for the nearest exit."

"That I don't believe for one second."

"I *was! Timidus Extremus,* that was me."

"When did you decide to pull out of it?"

"I didn't. When I saw how popular it was making me, I milked it for all it was worth."

I gave him a look and turned to Dad. "How about you?"

"I was shy in grade school, maybe even high school, a little. By the time I got to college, though, I figured if I really wanted something, I had to go after it, and after that the shyness took care of itself."

"Well, I think Eric's nice, and not because he stutters or he's shy, but because he returned my locket."

"I'm glad you got it back, honey," said Dad. "Your mother would have enjoyed seeing it on you."

I checked my E-mail that night. There was a message from Eric:

> I'm glad we finally connected and
> you're convinced I'm not a stalker. You

lost your Mom when you were five, and
that's about the time I started stuttering.
They're not the same, I know, but I
guess we've got that much in common:
A difficult five!
Eric alias CAY

I E-mailed back:

Hi, Eric alias CAY
Thanks for returning my locket.
I owe you one.
Alice

What happened the next day after school was so unexpected, so shocking, I couldn't believe it.

I'd heard some of the people on the stage crew talking about "earning your tattoo," and a few boys had joked about their own tattoos, but I figured it was a guy thing. Except for some extras who wander in from time to time, the stage crew for this production consisted of Molly and Faith and me, and four guys—Richard, Devon, Harry, and Ed. They're sort of a combination burly-funky-macho-artsy, and I think they've all got a body piercing somewhere. Friendly, though. Or so I thought.

When we met again the following week to start painting one of the backdrops for the outdoor scenes, I had just walked backstage with a paint-brush to ask where they wanted me to start, but I didn't see anyone there. Molly and Faith had gone to the home arts room to get the burlap pillow someone had stitched for us, but I was looking for Ed or Devon, who were doing the painting.

Suddenly the heavy black curtain at the back of the stage rippled, and then a couple of hands grabbed me, pulling me back behind it and down over somebody's knee. I was on my stomach, sprawled over a guy's leg.

"Hey, Alice, it's initiation time!" Ed said. "You gotta get your tattoo!"

My first thought was that it was a joke, but then I felt two hands tugging at my jeans, and my second thought was that I was about to be raped. Fingers were fumbling around in front, trying to unzip my fly because my jeans hardly budged, and when I started to kick and scream, I heard Devon's laugh, and a turpentine-smelling hand went over my mouth.

"Hey, hey, hey! Be good, now," Devon said.

I was struggling and trying to bite the fingers that were over my mouth, but somebody else appeared—Richard, I think—and they held me so tight, I couldn't move.

"Hey, guys, cut it out. She doesn't want it," came Harry's voice from the other side of the stage.

I was practically upside down, like a kid over her dad's knee, and my jeans and underpants were halfway down my bottom when somebody pressed something cold and hard against my right buttock, and then they let me go.

I tumbled to the floor, furious, and looked up at Ed and Devon and Richard, laughing at me and holding a rubber stamp belonging to the drama department, of the two Greek masks, comedy and tragedy, which they obviously had stamped on my butt.

"Are you out of your mind?" I yelled, scrambling to my feet and pulling my jeans back up. My face burned from both anger and humiliation. Molly appeared on the stage, Faith behind her, holding back the curtain. Molly stopped and stared at me, then at the guys.

"What were you *doing* to her?" Molly said.

"Initiation time, that's all!" Richard said. He was the tallest of the guys, lanky, and he didn't laugh, he leered.

"The Greek Tattoo!" Ed explained.

"Yeah? When they initiated me last year, they put it on my back. So where were you guys going to put it?" Molly said.

"*We* put it on her back!" Devon said innocently, and laughed.

I was pulling up my zipper as the side door of the stage opened, and the custodian came in. "Somebody yelling in here?" he asked, looking around. "You people have business back here?"

And when Devon said, "Yeah, we're painting sets," I didn't say a word. Neither did Faith or Molly. It was supposed to be all in fun. It was supposed to be a way of making me "one of the boys."

"Just forget about it, Alice, that's the way guys are," Faith said as the boys moved to the far side of the stage and opened the paint cans.

"It's not the way all guys are," I told her, thinking of Patrick. Of Eric. "And the ones that are shouldn't be allowed to get away with it. That was humiliating."

"They only meant it as a joke," she said. "When I was a freshman they put mine on a breast. I just laughed it off."

"Why are you defending them?" I asked.

"Well, what are *you* going to do? You're not going to report them, are you?" she said.

"I don't know," I answered. What I did know was that I hadn't been a "good sport," and I guess I figured that was embarrassment enough. It was over, and they wouldn't try it again. On me, anyway. So I didn't say anything.

When I told Dad that evening, though, he was furious.

"If that's not molestation, I don't know what is," he said.

"Stupidity," said Les.

"Al, had any of you talked about this before? Had the guys joked with you about getting this tattoo?"

"No! I didn't even know what initiation they were talking about. They just grabbed me!"

"Well, I'm going to call the superintendent," said Dad. "A freshman girl should not have to worry about being accosted by seniors."

"No! Dad, please don't!" I pleaded in horror.

Then he got angry at me. "You want to let something like that pass? No one reports it, and it will keep on happening to all the girls who come along after you."

"Al's right, though, Dad. She should handle it, not you," said Lester.

"What I'd *like* to do is pull the pants off those three guys and throw them out the window. Let them go outside buck naked and get them," I said.

"Well, you know you won't do that, so what *are* you going to do?" asked Dad.

"I'll think of something," I told him.

5

Out of the Woodwork

I still hadn't decided what I was going to do about it when I stayed after school the next day for our weekly staff meeting for *The Edge*. A part of me wished I'd handled it better—even laughed when the guys stamped my bottom. It would have made me a lot more popular.

The other part of me said that it was just this reaction—going along with the joke, no matter how humiliating—that kept this sort of hazing going. Nobody complained, nobody told, so it happened to the next batch of freshmen and the next and the next.

I'd thought about going to Mr. Ellis himself, but with all the other problems he was having getting the production off the ground, it was the last thing he wanted to hear. He'd probably say he'd take care of it, and nothing would happen. If I went to the student council, I'd be the poor little freshman telling on those big bad juniors and seniors, and if I went to the principal or superintendent, I'd have to make a formal complaint, they'd call in all the guys, and whatever happened, I'd be *persona non grata* on the stage crew. So I took it to the newspaper.

First I told Sara, our features editor, and before I'd even finished, she was rapping the table with her pen.

"Nick? Nick?" she kept saying till she got his attention. "You said we need more good lead stories, right? An exposé we can tie in with a good editorial? How about hazing?"

Nick looked a little pained. "Oh, come on, Sara."

"No, *you* come on!" she said. "We all know it happens, but Alice happens to know about it first-hand. Tell them, Alice."

So, in front of seven kids, I had to tell what happened to me behind the stage curtains the day before. A couple of the guys tried to hide a grin, but the girls were indignant. Nick, though, looked thoughtful.

"I'm thinking about the guy last year who got a tooth broken when they tried to force his head in the toilet—football initiation," he said. "The principal got involved, and we printed the new rules in the newspaper. That was supposed to stop the hazing, and obviously it hasn't. But how do we know this wasn't an isolated incident?"

Everybody started speaking at once. Each person there seemed to know of something that had happened to a friend.

"When I joined the girls' soccer team, they made me wear all my clothes inside out for a week," one of the sophomores said.

"That's not the kind of hazing we're talking about," said Sara.

We were all quiet for a moment.

"I know a guy in Arizona. . . ." The boy who started the sentence didn't finish. We turned and looked at him.

Tom Cordona was playing with a paper clip between his fingers. He didn't look up. "It was some guys on the wrestling team who did it to him. The broom-handle initiation," he said quietly.

"Oh, good grief!" said Sara, burying her head in her hands. "See what I mean, Nick? See how disgusting and humiliating . . ."

"Oh, man!" said our senior sports editor.

"Okay, listen," said Nick. "I think there's a story here, a lead story, but I don't want to go out on a limb with it if it didn't actually happen in our school. I want you people to ask everyone you know and get the facts. It can't just be something they've heard about happening to someone else. We need names and dates and we'll promise not to print them, just report what went on, see if we can't light a fire!"

• • •

What it lit, it seemed, was a forest fire. Even before we met again the following week, we were comparing notes and found out it was much bigger story than we'd thought. When kids knew we wouldn't use their names, we began hearing things we'd thought couldn't happen in our school. "Freshman initiation"—a group of guys circling a couple of freshmen girls in the parking lot, making them get down on their knees and unzip the boys' flies with their teeth; a boy who had to walk around all day with his fly open; a girl who had to crawl through a lineup of guys who paddled her; a boy who had to wear girls' underwear for a day; the girl who had to goose five guys.

We sat around the table in the journalism room and stared at one another when we realized what we had. These weren't just happening in Arizona or New York or Michigan or California, they were happening right here in Maryland in our school. To our students. And nobody, except the guy who had his tooth broken last year and whose dad had taken the incident to the school board, had complained. Everyone wanted to be a "good sport." We all had sort of swept it under the rug. No more.

"It's sexual and it's degrading, and I don't like the two put together," said Sara.

Miss Ames, our sponsor, agreed. She gave her

okay to do a story on it. Taking all of the information we'd gathered, Nick and Sara wrote the lead
article, but we used the names of the entire staff
in the byline, because we'd all contributed something, and we wanted to show that we were all
behind it.

It blew the roof off the school. The superintendent called us into his office and wanted details,
names, and dates, but our adviser sided with us
and said we didn't have to disclose them. It was a
serious problem and had to be addressed now to
stop future hazing.

The following week there was a school assembly,
and the principal announced a new set of rules. It
was clear, he said, that some forms of hazing were
all in fun and helped create a feeling of belonging
in a group. Things like being sent out on a scav-
enger hunt to get weird stuff, or going around
with your club's name painted on your forehead.
But no hazing of any kind, anywhere, was allowed
unless it was cleared first with a coach or sponsor.
Unauthorized hazing would lead to expulsion.

We all felt great! We went to Starbucks after
school and celebrated. Sam Mayer, one of the
paper's photographers, gave me a hug. "Nice going,
Alice," he said. Sara and Nick were pleased, too. I
wasn't too happy about the fact that Sara kept referring to it as "her" idea, but I guess when you're a

lowly freshman you have to pay your dues and let the big guns get the glory.

"That's the way to do it, kiddo! Take it to the newspaper!" Lester told me when I showed him the article in *The Edge*.

"Get an extra copy for me," said Dad. "I want to send it to Sylvia. No, get three. Let's send one to Sally and Milt, and one to your uncles in Tennessee."

Patrick complimented me on the article, and so did Penny. I was feeling so super-confident of myself that I found I could even talk to her as though we'd been friends forever. I didn't have to go around the rest of my life known as "Patrick's ex."

"I'll bet you guys on the newspaper have some interesting staff meetings," Penny said to me. "There are probably all sorts of things that go on in school you don't even put in the paper. Right?"

"Well, some," I said.

We were at lunch, and she had broken her giant-sized cookie in two and put half on my tray. Patrick never ate with us because he didn't have time for lunch. He grabbed a sandwich between classes. "You going to major in journalism?"

"I'm not sure yet."

"You'd be good at it," Penny said.

"I've been thinking about psychology."

"Really? I think I'm interested in advertising, and there's a lot of psychology in that," she said.

Gwen liked my article, too. She's the friend who's helped me with math and algebra more times than I can count. "Way to go, girl!" she said.

But the two people I would most like to have shared it with didn't say much of anything. Every time our eyes met, Liz and Pam were suddenly deep in conversation with each other, and it was all so phony. They laughed and joked with the other kids, but if the spotlight fell on me, they started giggling over their own little secrets.

I remembered a column in the *Washington Post* about problems that parents were having with their children, and one of the things it said was that sometimes when a child is behaving the worst, he's most in need of love. Maybe you didn't have to be a child. Maybe no matter how old you were, you needed love most when you were the most disagreeable, which was the way Pamela and Elizabeth had been acting toward me lately. And maybe it was up to me to make the first move.

On Friday night, when I saw a light up in Elizabeth's room at eight o'clock, I figured she was home for the evening, and took a chance.

I wrote a note and went over to her house. When her dad answered the door, I asked if he'd take the note up to Liz, and I'd wait. I could tell he was glad to see me, that he'd wondered what was wrong between us.

The note said:

Liz, if I have done or said anything to hurt you, I'm sorry. I still like you best in the whole wide world, and really miss you. Can I come up? Alice

It took about two minutes, but finally her dad came back down and said it was okay for me to go up. When I got to her room, she was crying. I started to cry, too, and we stood in her doorway, crying and hugging. She had three pimples on her face now, and if ever she needed to be loved, it was then. What I didn't know was that Pamela was on her way over to spend the night with Liz, and she got there a few minutes later. I gave her the same type of note I'd given Liz, all ready to go in my pocket. She didn't cry but she hugged me, and we sat facing one another on Elizabeth's twin beds with the white ruffled spreads and canopies, and talked it out.

"Pamela, do you remember back in seventh grade, how you were always telling me I wasn't part of the 'seventh-grade experience' unless I joined some clubs, got active? I'm just taking your advice, that's all. Trying to get into things more. It always seemed easier for you than for me," I said.

"But you're doing so *many* things!" Elizabeth protested.

"I know. But Liz, remember when you were taking ballet and tap and piano and I don't know what all! I didn't shut you out. I've been a wallflower for so long, I'm just trying to make up for lost time," I said, wanting to make her laugh.

"Yes, but you . . . you don't have to be so stuck on yourself," Elizabeth said.

I was surprised. "Am I? Is that the way I seem? Because I don't think of myself like that at all. I'm just a lowly stagehand."

"Yeah, but that newspaper thing," said Pamela. "We've been friends a lot longer than you've been in ninth grade, remember. And when you say you'll show up and you don't, and you don't answer E-mails . . ."

I could see now how I must have appeared to them. "I know, and it's going to get worse from here until the production's over," I said. "Between the newspaper and *Fiddler on the Roof* and the Melody Inn and my homework on weekends, I'm going down for the third time, guys. Can't you see me through this? I really, really need you."

"Maybe it's a good thing you don't have a boyfriend this semester, Alice," said Elizabeth. "At least *we* can understand."

"But do you?" I said. "Things are going to be

really awful for the next few weeks, but we could get together over spring vacation and do something. Easter comes early this year."

"All right," said Pamela. "But it's got to be something really wild."

"Something we've never done before!" said Elizabeth bravely.

"Right!" I said. We all laughed.

"Oh, guys, it's so good to be back again," I told them. "I needed you so bad a couple of weeks ago. I wanted to call you, but I was afraid you wouldn't talk to me."

"What happened?" they both asked together.

If there is one thing that makes your girlfriends sympathetic, it's something bad happening to you, I've decided. "I was backstage getting ready to paint one of the sets," I said, "when some of the guys grabbed me, turned me over, and pulled down my jeans."

Elizabeth almost went catatonic. "They *didn't!*" she gasped.

"You mean . . . that story in the newspaper . . . about putting a rubber stamp on your bottom, was *you?*"

I felt embarrassed all over again. In answer, I stood up, turned around, and pulled my jeans halfway down. The stamp mark with the two masks had faded some, but the permanent ink was still visible.

When I sat down again, they were both speechless.

"You mean . . . ?" Pamela said finally. "You mean they actually held you down and pulled your jeans completely off?"

"No, just down far enough to put the stamp."

"Exactly how far was that?" Elizabeth said. "Turn around again."

"Now, Liz . . ."

"What were you wearing underneath?"

"Underpants, of course!"

"See-through?" asked Elizabeth. She has to know the details.

"My gosh, what does it matter?" said Pamela. "The underwear went down, too! Alice, I'd be furious!"

"Well, I was."

"But . . . what if . . . what if you'd been having your period and were wearing a pad!" Elizabeth went on in horror. "What if you had pimples on your butt or . . . ?"

Leave it to Elizabeth. If you don't provide enough details, she'll offer some of her own.

"Exactly," I said. "But even if I'd been wearing French underwear and looked like a million bucks, no one had the right to embarrass me like that."

"What did you do?" asked Pamela.

"Everything I could think of. I yelled and kicked and bit, but it didn't do any good. There were three of them. Harry was the only one who didn't take part, but he didn't make them stop, either." I was surprised to find my mouth sagging down at the corners. "I wanted so bad to call you guys that night. . . ."

We all hugged again.

"You know," I said. "Being best friends means we've got to be there for each other when things are going good, too. It's easy to comfort someone when they're down, but sometimes when we're up, we need to know we haven't lost our best friends. Listen, Pam, you may not believe me, but your voice is every bit as good as some of the girls who tried out. Next year you might get a starring role. Wouldn't you want Liz and me there, cheering you on?"

"If that ever happens, sure, I would," she said. "Listen, Alice. I'm sorry. I've been a toad, and I know it."

"Me, too," said Elizabeth.

"A toad?" I said, laughing. "A *toad?*"

"**T**otally **O**bnoxious **A**nytime **D**ame," Pamela explained, laughing.

"Okay, you want to know a secret?" I said. They were all ears. "I found out who CAY is."

"Who?" they cried.

"A guy in my biology class. Eric Fielding."

They each tried to remember.

"Blond?" asked Pamela. I nodded.

"He's cute, but he stutters, doesn't he?"

"So?"

"Gosh, he never says two words to anyone!" said Elizabeth. "He's in my history class. Did you meet him at the statue or what?"

I told them about Mom's locket and how he had found it on the floor.

"It takes him forever and a day to say anything," said Elizabeth. "The teacher hardly ever calls on him because it's so painful to listen to him. He's worse in class."

"A lot more painful for him, I imagine," I said.

"So did he talk? Did he say anything?" asked Pamela.

"Of course. He walked me to my next class."

"Are you going out with him?" Pamela asked.

"We're just friends," I said. "So what's happening with you guys? Tell me everything."

"Have you got all night?" asked Elizabeth.

"Well, actually, yes. Yes, I do."

"Why don't you stay over, then? Pamela is."

"I haven't got any stuff with me."

"Use ours," said Pamela. "Don't go home, and we'll see what we can dig up for you."

I laughed. "Okay," I said. "Let me call Dad."

They rounded up toothpaste and deodorant and a comb and pj's for me, and we hunkered down on Elizabeth's twin beds. Pamela told me how her voice lessons were going and how her dad's dating a nurse. Elizabeth said she was feeling mad at her therapist lately, but her therapist says it's normal, and at least she's getting along better with her folks now.

Then Nathan toddled into the room in his jammies to kiss Elizabeth good night, and we made him kiss us all. We got down on the floor and growled at him and chased him around the beds on our knees, watching his short little legs churn across the floor and listening to his excited squeals, till Mrs. Price came in to rescue him.

"You'll have him so worked up, he'll never go to sleep," she said, laughing. "Are you staying all night, Alice? I could bring up the cot."

"Tonight we're going to push the two beds together and all sleep in one big bed," Elizabeth said.

"We've got a lot to talk about," said Pamela.

Another person who had a lot to talk about was Aunt Sally. I should have known what would happen if Dad sent her a copy of *The Edge* with that article on hazing in it. I was quietly eating some chocolate grahams one day after school when Aunt Sally called from Chicago.

"Alice, I am *shocked!* Simply *shocked!*" she said.

"I want you taken out of that school and enrolled in a private academy, and your Uncle Milt and I have the money to pay for it if necessary."

"Uh . . . Aunt Sally—" I began.

"If Marie knew that her little Alice was going to a school where girls have to get down on their knees in the parking lot and unzip boys' pants with their *teeth* . . . *!* The *humiliation,* not to mention what it does to teeth! I could hardly sleep last night from worrying about you."

"I'm sure that—"

"And that poor girl who had her pants pulled down in front of a gang of leering boys. She'll be traumatized for life. She'll probably never marry because of it and, if she does, she'll be one of those women who undresses in the closet."

"What?" I said. Once in a while I actually learn something from Aunt Sally. And then, playing innocent, I asked, "Is that what it means to 'come out of the closet'?"

"No, no, no," Aunt Sally said hastily. "I'm speaking about the misguided souls who are too shy to undress in front of their husbands even after fifty years."

"Well, I happen to know the girl who had her jeans pulled down, Aunt Sally, and she was pretty upset for a while, but she's getting over it," I said. "It was largely on account of her that we published the article."

"You never know about these things, though," said Aunt Sally. "A girl could experience something like that and the effects might not show up for five or ten years." I thought of Elizabeth and how that was probably true. "The best thing you can do for your friend, Alice, is encourage her to get her feelings out, even if they're irrational and against all men in general. She shouldn't just sit around and let them fester."

"I'll remember to tell her that, Aunt Sally," I said. "But meanwhile, the principal has gotten real strict about enforcing the rules, and anyone who does any unauthorized hazing could get expelled."

"I should hope so!" she said. "But anytime you feel you want to change schools, dear, Uncle Milt and I could help out."

"I really appreciate it," I said.

"And keep an eye on that girlfriend," she added.

Lester came home just then, and lumbered out to the kitchen for a beer. As he leaned over to get one out of the fridge, I reached out with my foot and gave him a little kick in the behind.

He reared up. "What was *that* for?"

"For mankind in general," I said.

"*Why?*"

"So I don't sit around and fester," I told him.

6

Spring Surprises

Probably because I hadn't scrubbed the bathroom or kitchen for three weeks, Dad suddenly noticed how grimy our house had become. No one had hassled me because they knew I had to stay at school late most afternoons, if not for the stage crew, then for the newspaper. Consequently I was excused from all cleaning and cooking until *Fiddler on the Roof* was over. But because the bathroom and kitchen were so dirty, Dad and Les had sort of let the vacuuming and dusting go, too, and the fact was, our house was filthy.

"I can't let Sylvia move into this place looking the way it does," Dad said the week before spring break. "We've got to do something."

"We could start with a wrecking crew," said Les, stuffing the last third of a doughnut into his mouth as he finished his coffee.

"A constructive suggestion, please," said Dad.

"A fumigation company? Dust-Busters?"

Dad ignored him. "The drapes have to be taken down and cleaned, the bathroom and kitchen repainted—I should really have my bedroom redecorated. It looks like a hermit's been living in there."

"A hermit has," I said fondly.

"Hey, Dad, leave a little something for Sylvia to do. She'll probably want to change things around, anyway," said Les.

"Well, the place has to be clean, at least," Dad said.

"I can help out over spring vacation," I promised.

"What about closets?" asked Dad. "Are we supposed to clean closets, too? I can't remember that Marie ever said."

"Let's don't go overboard now," Les told him.

"And the inside of the oven. Now I know you're supposed to clean that."

"Why?" said Les. "Just turn it on to five hundred degrees, and the heat will kill all the germs."

"What else do you clean?" asked Dad, looking at me. "Are you supposed to clean the inside of the dryer? The dishwasher? How is a man supposed to know all this stuff?"

"You could always call Aunt Sally," I chirped helpfully.

"No!" Dad and Lester bellowed together. We all knew that one phone call to Chicago and Aunt Sally would be on the next plane, broom and bucket in hand. And she'd probably start by making us clean the broom and the bucket.

I'd begun sitting by Eric in biology. We can sit wherever we like, but once we start a project with someone, we have to stay at that particular table till it's finished.

"You want t-to d-do something Friday nnnn-night—celebrate a week of vacation?" he asked.

"Sure," I said. "What would you like to do?"

"Sail around the world, for one," he said.

"Sounds good to me," I told him, and he laughed. I noticed that sometimes he stuttered and sometimes he didn't. Or he would repeat the first letter of a word one time and drag it out another. It was always worse, it seemed, when he first began a conversation. After he got into it, he often didn't. He also seemed to stutter on particular letters, like P and B. But after awhile I wasn't listening to his stutter. I was listening to what he had to say. To a person who stutters, though, I suppose he thinks we only focus on the stutter.

"Would you like to see a movie at Wheaten P-Plaza? The new T-Tom Hanks movie?" he asked.

"That sounds fun," I said. I knew, from the first note he'd sent me, that he lived out by Dale Drive, and we lived in exactly the opposite direction. "Want me to meet you there?"

"Okay. But I'll t-take you home," he said. "If you d-don't mind the bbbbb-bus."

"Sure. What time?"

"I'll E-mail you," he said.

One thing I had discovered about Eric: He never called me on the phone.

Meanwhile, Elizabeth, Pamela, and I were trying to think of something we could do over spring break to "express ourselves," as Liz had put it. "Something that is really, truly us."

The question, of course, was what we really, truly were. Not only were the three of us different from each other, but we changed from day to day, and so did our moods. One of us might be up and the other two down, or vice versa.

"Maybe we could get jobs as go-go girls for the week," said Pamela. "Dance on customers' tables." She grinned at me, noticing Elizabeth's change of expression. "Or we could even get hired as lap dancers."

"As what?" said Elizabeth.

"You dance in customer's laps," I told her.

"*What?* You actually stand up on a man's legs and—"

"You sit," said Pamela, grinning. "You sit facing him on his lap with your legs on either side of him."

Elizabeth looked from Pamela to me.

"And wiggle around," I explained.

A look of horror crossed Elizabeth's face. "That's obscene!"

"That's the point," said Pamela.

We decided not to apply as go-go dancers. We thought of taking a moonlight cruise—just the three of us—on a dinner boat on the Potomac, but that cost more than any of us wanted to spend.

It was Elizabeth, finally, who came up with something wacky, if not entirely wild. She saw a notice on the community bulletin board at the library that high school students were invited to dress up as their favorite storybook characters and read to groups of children at the Martin Luther King Library between nine and five during spring vacation.

"Let's do it!" said Pamela. "I want to dress up like Scarlet O'Hara."

"And read *Gone with the Wind* to preschoolers?" I said.

We finally decided on Huck Finn for me, a monster from *Where the Wild Things Are* for Elizabeth, and *Amelia Bedelia* for Pamela. So in addition to having to find props for *Fiddler on the Roof,* finishing my last "behind-the-scenes" article for *The Edge,* doing school assignments, working on Saturday at the Melody Inn, helping Dad clean the house, and going out with Eric, I had to put together a costume. I thought my head would pop off.

I think we were all glad for a week's break before the production. We'd have three weeks after we got back to do the final rehearsals and get things shipshape, but for now we needed a rest.

I told Dad I was meeting Eric at the cinema at Wheaton Plaza.

"Just make sure he sees you home," he said. "I don't want you coming home after dark by yourself."

I took the bus to Wheaton Plaza, and Eric was waiting for me at the box office. He had our tickets.

"I was afraid you m-might stand me up to p-pay me back for that first t-time," he said, grinning at me as we went inside.

And there, standing right in front of the refreshment stand, were Patrick and Penny, buying an extra-large tub of popcorn.

"Hey, Eric! How's it going?" Patrick said. And then he saw me. "Alice!"

"Hi, Patrick. Hi, Penny," I said. "Everybody's out celebrating our week of freedom, huh?"

"Looks that way," said Penny.

They went on inside, and Eric bought popcorn and drinks for us. I was glad he didn't suggest sitting with Patrick and Penny. We sat halfway down on one side, Eric put the popcorn between us, and when the tub was gone and our eyes were on the screen, he casually put his arm around the back of my seat and I noticed that when something really funny happened, he'd squeeze my shoulder when he laughed.

I felt comfortable with Eric, just as I had with Patrick, and discovered that was one thing I looked for in a guy: I wanted to feel comfortable with him, know that I could be myself. That I didn't have to worry about what he might do or say next.

When it was over, he suggested we go to the Pizza Hut, so we did. I told him we'd split the check, and we got a table along one side where it wasn't too noisy, and just talked over Coke and a couple slices of pizza, triple cheese.

"We're moving in June," he said.

"You *are?*"

"Yeah. Dad's with IBM, and they're mmm-moving us to Dallas."

"Darn!" I said. "Just when I start liking a guy, he up and moves away." I surprised even myself. I guess I felt I could say it because he'd be leaving anyway.

I could tell it pleased him, though. He reached across and put his hand over mine. "I g-guess that n-note I sent you was pretty c-c-c-c-"

It seemed as though the word just wouldn't come out. If I knew what he was trying to say, I might have said it for him. But his face was beginning to color, his eyes began blinking faster, and he jerked his head slightly as though trying to shake the word from his mouth.

Finally I smiled at him and said, "Need help?"

"N-N-No," he said. "C-Crazy. That's the word. I g-guess you thought that n-note was pretty crazy."

"Well, it had me wondering," I said. "I'll admit it was different, and it certainly got my attention."

He still had hold of my hand. "Thanks," he said.

"For what?"

"For not finishing the sentence for me b-back there. P-People always do that. They think they're helping, but it just mmm-makes me feel like I'm five years old."

"You're welcome," I said, and smiled back.

"So n-now that we broke the ice, c-can we get together again b-before I move?"

"Of course," I said.

We took the bus back to my house. Les was out

for the evening, but Dad was home, and he invited Eric in and talked a little bit about the kind of work his dad did. He offered to drive Eric home, but Eric said he'd rather take the bus.

I walked him back out on the porch, and he kissed me. A light, friendly, platonic kind of kiss, and then, because I smiled at him, maybe, he kissed me again, not quite so platonic that time.

"This was a good way to begin vacation," I told him. "I had a great time."

He squeezed my arm. "So did I," he said.

Elizabeth called the Martin Luther King Library in the District, and they gave us the ten-to-two time slot. Elizabeth would read *Where the Wild Things Are* to groups of preschoolers, Pamela would read one of the *Amelia Bedelia* books to the first through third graders, and I would read something from *Tom Sawyer* or *Huckleberry Finn* to fourth and fifth graders. And we each had to perform four times.

The fun part was that Mrs. Price drove us to the Metro each morning, and we rode the subway downtown in costume. What was really wild was that Washington, D.C., is full of tourists around Easter, and when we'd get on the subway in Silver Spring, there would be loads of kids and their parents going down to the Smithsonian museums, and suddenly kids would start shouting, "Mom!

Look! A monster!" Or, "There's Amelia Bedelia!" Or, "Hi, Huck. How ya doin'?"

We were having a blast. Pamela had on a plain blue dress and a white apron; a hat, with her hair fashioned into bangs peeking out beneath the brim; and black shoes. A. BEDELIA was embroidered on her apron, just so kids would know.

Elizabeth looked great in a fleece costume her mom had made for her, with long claws in the pads of the hands and feet, large eyes resting above her own eyes, and fangs. What it was was a teen-sized sleeper with a zipper front, and because she couldn't do anything with her hands, we had to get a fare card for her, hold a tissue so she could blow her nose, and help her get the costume off when she had to go to the bathroom. Once, when Huck Finn was blowing the monster's nose, people started snapping our picture. As we were heading for the library after we'd left the Metro, a photographer for the *Post* happened to be driving by, and he stopped his car and took our picture. It was on the first page of the Metro section the next day.

Going back home that first day, we realized we were more effective if we acted the parts. We'd get on the Metro and while Huck Finn slouched down in his seat with his straw hat at a tipsy angle, and corncob pipe in his mouth, Amelia

Bedelia sat prim and proper with her hands in her lap, while the monster had a ball going up and down the aisle, showing her claws and roaring her terrible roar, while kids laughed and shrieked and hid behind their mothers. I think some of the tourists thought we were hired by the Metro to provide entertainment during spring vacation.

"It was great!" I told Dad and Lester that night. "I never saw Elizabeth cut loose like that. I guess it was because she could hide behind that monster suit."

"And how were the audiences?" Dad asked. I was trying to read Dad's mood, to see if he was even listening to me, because Sylvia was supposed to have called him the night before and she didn't. She'd be traveling around England during Easter vacation, she'd told us, and he wanted to know how she had liked Bath, the place she was to visit first.

"The audiences were terrific!" I told him. "It's nice to be having fun and doing something useful at the same time."

It was a good thing Les brought home Thai food that night, because I was too tired to help cook, and Dad had just taken down all our drapes and curtains and sent them to the cleaners. I put on a pair of leggings and an old shirt and would have eaten whatever was on the table, I was so tired, and Dad was in his sweats. But we were all feeling mellow—Dad, because he'd made a dent in spring cleaning; Les, because he was going to a concert with his philosophy instructor later in the week; and me, because it had been a really fun day, and Liz and Pam and I were friends again.

Dad had just stood up to get the ice cream from the fridge when the doorbell rang. *Eric?* I thought, and hoped it wasn't him, because I was too tired to see anyone except my family.

"I'll get it," Dad said.

"There were some boys from a football team out selling raffle tickets, Dad," Les called. "Why don't you just not answer?"

But Dad's never been able to do that, so he padded to the door in his stocking feet, taking the mint chocolate chip with him.

I heard the door open, and then what sounded like a cry from Dad, followed by, "Sylvia!"

"Oh, Ben!"

Les and I scooted out from the table and peered down the hall. My father had his arms around Sylvia Summers. All I could see of her was her light brown hair against Dad's face, her black slacks and turquoise sweater, because her lips were probably against Dad's, her arms were around his neck, he was hugging her close to him, while a cab pulled away out front.

I quietly tiptoed out into the hall, rescued the mint chocolate chip from where it had fallen beside Sylvia's suitcase, and took it back to the kitchen.

7

Conversation

Les and I both finished our ice cream before Dad came up for air. We just sat at the kitchen table grinning at each other, and finally Dad and Sylvia walked into the kitchen. She looked flushed and girlish, and Dad had the look of a little boy in love, lipstick on his chin.

"So . . . are you going to elope?" Les asked, and that made us all laugh.

"I really intended to spend spring vacation traveling around England," Sylvia explained, sitting down at the table, "but as I was packing I thought, *I don't want to do this without Ben; I don't want to see all these places until I can share them with him.* And suddenly I knew that what I wanted most was to spend my two weeks back here. I called the airline, and they said a plane was leaving in three hours. I never packed so fast in my life. And here I am."

"Oh, Sylvia!" I said, jumping up and hugging her.

All I could think of, of course, was where she was going to sleep. And then Dad said, "Let me take a quick shower and I'll drive you over."

While Dad was upstairs, Sylvia explained that the woman who had been renting her house had decided to go to Syracuse the month before. "I'm anxious to see my place, drive my car, see how my plants survived the winter. . . ." She looked at me and smiled. "I guess I was just plain homesick. For Ben. For all of you."

"Are you going to stay?" I asked.

"Oh, no. I've got to go back. A contract is a contract. But July will be here before we know it. I can hardly wait."

"Neither can I!" I said happily.

"I don't know if I'm ready for all that hullabaloo," Les joked. "The ribbons, the flowers, the invitations, the clothes, the photographers, the. . . ."

"How do you know, Les? You've never been married," I said.

"I've been best man at too many weddings. I know," he said. "Besides, weddings are like infections. They're contagious. Once dad gets caught up in it, we'll all be caught up in it." And then he said, "Seriously, Sylvia, we're all glad you're back. He's a new man when you're around."

"He's the same old Ben to me," she said, and smiled some more.

She ate ice cream with us while we told her all our news and she told us more about Chester. And then Dad came down in a fresh shirt, his hair washed and combed, and as he threw on his jacket he said, "I don't know just when I'll be back. Carry on!" And, with his arm around Sylvia, they went out to his car.

I looked at Les.

"Shut up," he said.

"*What?* All I was going to say was—"

"Don't even go there," said Les.

I grinned. "I think we should have given Dad a curfew."

Les smiled back. "It wouldn't have done one bit of good."

Of course I had to go right to the phone and call Elizabeth, then Pamela.

"Where is she going to sleep?" asked Elizabeth. She sounded just like me.

"Dad's driving her back to her place."

"Oh, Alice! Isn't this exciting! In four more months you'll be calling her 'Mother.' You never guessed, did you, when you walked in her English class back in seventh grade that someday she'd be marrying your father?"

"No. And Dad never guessed it, either. Boy, he

was so lonely back then, Liz. Isn't it amazing how fast your life can turn around?"

I stayed up late watching an old *ER* rerun with Lester, and then I conked out. Around eleven-thirty I felt someone shaking my shoulder and opened my eyes to see that I had fallen across Lester's lap, one arm on the couch cushion, one dangling on the floor, my feet at an awkward angle on the rug.

"Hey, Al, go to bed," he told me. He'd turned the TV off, and I realized I must have been asleep for a while, because my neck was stiff. I slowly unwound my feet and sat up.

"Is Dad home yet?" I asked, flopping back against the cushions.

"Not yet."

"I just had the weirdest dream, Les! I"—I yawned, then snapped my jaws together—"I dreamed that there were all these people—I don't know where I was, but we were in this big crowd, and you were chasing me, only I don't know why, and Dad and Sylvia were there but they didn't try to stop you, and I realized I knew how to fly. I climbed up this tall ladder . . . no, maybe it was a tower . . . and I got to the top and was so sure that if I just put my arms straight out and flapped them up and down, I would fly. I just knew it. And you got to the top of the tower and I said I was going to jump off and you said no, wait, and all the people were looking up and I jumped . . . and then I woke up. I wanted to see if I could do it, but I woke up! I was so sure!"

I yawned again and hugged myself with my arms, my eyes half closed. "Why were you chasing me?" I asked.

"How the heck should I know? It was *your* dream."

"What do you think it meant?"

"Aha!" Lester stroked his chin and took on the voice of a Viennese psychiatrist. "Und vat ver you vearing?"

"Uh . . . shorts, I think. And a T-shirt; I'm not sure."

"Un vat vass I vearing?"

"I don't know. Jeans, maybe."

"Vat iss your first azzoziation to my chazing you?"

I thought about it. "I don't think I was scared. I just wanted to show you I could fly."

"Aha!" said Lester. And then, in his normal voice, "Obviously, you've got a crush on your older brother and—"

"I do *not!*" I said.

"And to gain his approval, you wanted to show that you could do something extraordinary. In this case, that you could fly."

"I thought dreams were supposed to be predictions of things to come."

"You want predictions? Okay. You are going to do something scary that you have never done before. How's that?"

"And? What happens, Les?"

"You fall flat on your face."

"*Les*-ter!"

"So go to bed, Al," he said. "I'm tired." He got up and began turning off lights.

"You're going to leave one on for Dad, aren't you?" I said.

"Oh. Right." He left a light on by the phone in the hallway, and we both went upstairs. I put on my pajamas and fell into bed. I slept soundly till about two-fifteen. I was desperately thirsty from all the corn chips Les and I had eaten, so I got up to get a drink. The light was still on downstairs. I glanced at Dad's room. The door was open, his bed untouched.

I was in my Huck Finn costume the next morning and just getting ready to leave when Dad came downstairs in his robe, looking very sleepy. Les glanced up from his coffee and raised one eyebrow at Dad, smiling.

"Guess I overslept," Dad said, reaching for a mug from the cupboard, trying to keep his eyes open and look more awake than he was.

"And . . . uh . . . what time did *you* get in last night?" Les said.

"Pretty late, I'm afraid. We had a lot to talk about."

"Uh-huh," I said.

"She sure took us by surprise, didn't she?" said Dad.

Les cleared his throat and looked at me. "I don't know, Al. Do you think we should have some rules around here? A curfew, maybe?"

"I don't think that eleven o'clock would be at all unreasonable," I said.

"And of course we need to know where you'll be, Dad, and who you're with," Les continued.

"And you have to promise to call if you see you're going to be late," I said.

Dad just chuckled. "Go ahead," he said. "Have your fun. But you can't get a rise out of me, because I'm mellow."

"Cool, you mean," said Lester.

"Yes," said Dad, smiling still. "Very cool indeed."

The Metro was really crowded the next day. Some big event was going on in Washington, and there was standing room only. It wasn't too difficult for Pamela and me to maneuver in our costumes, but Elizabeth, in her monster suit, with footpads and claws, didn't have such an easy time of it. Half the stuff on her costume was attached by Velcro, and she didn't want to lose any of it. Of course, she could have carried it in a bag and put it on once we got to the library, but that would have ruined the fun.

We had to squeeze to make sure we all got on the same car, and when the train stopped at the next station, everyone had to move back even more. The closer we got to downtown Washington, though, the more people got off, and when there was space enough to breathe again, I looked at Elizabeth and said, "Liz, your goggle eyes are missing."

"What?" She reached up and felt the space above her own eyes where the huge goggle eyes of the monster were supposed to be. They were gone.

We immediately started looking all around as people smiled at us and children pointed, and then Pam said, "Oh, look!"

A very dignified man in a gray pinstripe suit had a briefcase in one hand, and was holding on to the handrail overhead with the other. He was standing near the front of the car, and the band of Velcro with the goggle eyes on it was stuck to the bottom of his suit coat.

"Pamela!" Elizabeth gasped.

"Go get them!" I said. "The next stop is Metro Center, and half the car will be getting off."

Someone moved forward in the aisle, brushing past the man in the pinstripe suit, and now the goggle eyes had slipped down to the dignified man's pants and seemed glued to his bottom. A little boy saw them and began laughing.

"Liz, go!" I said again.

Elizabeth lurched forward as the train began to slow, her footpads flopping on the floor of the car, and when she reached the gentleman she said, "Excuse me, sir, but I believe my eyes are on the seat of your pants." And she bent down and peeled them off while he stared at her incredulously. Two rows of people who were watching burst into laughter, and then the man laughed, too.

He turned and looked at Pamela and me, and then Elizabeth again. "You look like something out of a book I used to read to my son when he was little," he said. "'The night Max wore his wolf suit and made mischief of one kind or another, his mother called him wild thing. . . .'" He winked at us. "Maurice Sendak, I think," he said, and as the door opened, he stepped out onto the platform and into the crowd.

Sylvia and I went shopping the last day of spring vacation. Dad didn't feel he could take any more time away from the store, and Sylvia needed some things she couldn't find in England, so she asked if I would like to go to White Flint with her. When I got home from the library and changed clothes, she drove over from Kensington and picked me up, and we went to Bloomingdale's and Lord and Taylor's. I would have followed her wherever she went, lost in a trail of her wonderful perfume.

White Flint Mall is a fancier kind of mall than Wheaton Plaza, and it was having a strolling fashion show. Models walked around all three levels in clothes I wouldn't wear in a million years, and there were strolling musicians and a photographer taking people's pictures.

We had just bought some panty hose and a white jacket for Sylvia, and a couple of shirts for me, and were having tea and scones at a little table outside a restaurant on the top level when the musicians came over to play for us. One was playing an accordion and the other a violin, and they smiled at us—at Sylvia, mostly—as they played. And while we were listening, a photographer snapped our picture and gave Sylvia a number and an address in case she wanted to order a copy.

"I'm glad I came back over spring vacation," she said when he'd gone.

"I'm glad you came, too," I said. "I've never seen Dad so happy."

"And *I've* never *felt* so happy," she said. "I can't believe I'm so lucky to get a ready-made family. You know what it felt like today, shopping with you? As though I were with my sister again."

"She's out west, isn't she?"

"Yes. I almost feel guilty not going out there while I'm back, but I'll see her in just a few months when she comes for the wedding. We used to do everything together when we were growing up, and I miss that sometimes."

"What all did you do?" I asked.

"Well"—Sylvia took another sip of her tea— "let's see. She's a couple years younger than I am. I wheeled her around in my doll buggy once. I remember that because I accidentally tipped it, and over she went. I taught her to play hopscotch. We sang duets together. We curled each other's hair, I don't know. . . . Some girls fight with their sisters, but we were really close."

"It's good you remember so much," I told her.

"What do you remember of your mother?"

"Not very much. But I think she and Dad loved each other a lot." I wondered suddenly if I should have said that. Or *why* I'd said that. Why did my brain think of what might upset someone the most and then direct my mouth to say it? But it didn't seem to bother her a bit. If anything, she liked to hear it.

"That's a good sign," she said. "I don't think I would be comfortable marrying a man who had been miserable in a marriage. This means he liked being married, and knows it will probably make him happy again."

"But don't . . . don't you want him to forget about Mom when he's with you?" I asked.

Sylvia cocked her head and looked at me with her blue-green eyes. "Why on earth would I expect that of him, Alice? Marie was such a big part of his life. There were some men in my life who I like to think about now and then. Little things that remind me of them. Ben and I like to share these memories with each other."

"What?" I said. "You actually *tell* each other you're thinking of someone else?"

She laughed. "Why not? There's a lot of difference between just thinking about a person and actually going out and *being* with another person—in a close, intimate way, I mean. That kind of relationship is reserved for your dad."

I sighed. "It sounds very adult to me. I'm not sure I could ever feel that mature about things. I mean, that I wouldn't mind if a guy I was with was thinking about another girl. To tell the truth, I don't understand a lot about love."

Sylvia chuckled and divided the last scone between us. "To tell the truth, I don't, either. But

we don't have to, you know. All we need to do is
enjoy it."

She went back two days before her school
reopened after spring break. I thought Dad would
be really down, but he wasn't. He seemed just as
happy as he was before, as though her love would
keep him going for the next few months until she
was in his arms again. I was almost jealous of
her—that she could make him feel that good.

When I kissed him that night, I played our little
game. "Like me?" I asked, rubbing his nose with
mine.

"Hm?" he said.

I tried again. "Like me?"

"Rivers." He grinned.

"Love me?"

As I said the words, however, the phone rang and
he sprang up to answer. It was someone collecting
used clothes for Purple Heart. When he came back
to the sofa, he said, "I thought it might be Sylvia
saying that her flight was canceled or something."

I repeated the phrase. "Love me?"

"Of course," he said.

"No, Dad! You're supposed to say 'oceans'!" I
told him.

"Of course. Oceans," he said. But he *could* have
put a little more feeling into it.

8

Production

We had three weeks after we returned from spring vacation to get the musical in shape. The cast worked to master their lines, the orchestra to fine-tune the music, the stage crew to get all the props and costumes. The production was to run for four nights—Friday and Saturday of one week, and Friday and Saturday the next. Dad gave me both Saturdays off from the Melody Inn, and a couple of the teachers even gave us an extra week to do our assignments.

The stage crew was down to the nitty-gritty now—no goofing off. Because I was matter-of-fact with the three guys who had "tattooed" me, they began to treat me okay. Harry, in fact—the fourth guy on the stage crew—apologized for not stopping the other boys when they'd pulled my jeans down. "Next time I see something like that," he said, "I'll do more than just tell them to stop."

"Let's hope there's no next time for anybody," I said.

A week before the first performance, Mr. Ellis told us that the entire cast and crew were invited to the home of Kurt Weinstein, the guy who was playing Tevye, to observe the Sabbath. At first they said only the cast members were to go, then they said everyone was invited, that the Weinsteins had a big house. Some of the kids couldn't make it, but the rest of us, maybe thirty in all, sat or stood around the Weinsteins' family room on a Friday night, meeting the parents and grandparents who spent the Sabbath with them every week, as well as the ninety-eight-year-old great-grandfather.

We shared stories and listened to the grandfather's hesitant account of a grammar-school production he was in after his family came over from Russia.

"And because I did not still know the English well, I was given no lines to say, but was to play the part of the mule," he told us, and we laughed.

Kurt's father studied his watch and, at sundown, signaled that the Sabbath candles were to be lit. We all squeezed into the living and dining rooms, where two long tables had been placed end to end, extending from one room into the other. The meal had been cooked, and the heavy silver candelabrum polished. Kurt's mother, wearing a beautiful silk blouse, lit two candles, and Mr. Weinstein explained that they were symbols of peace, freedom, and light, which the Sabbath brings to the human soul. Copies of the blessings had been given to each of us, and we watched in fascination as the candlelight flickered and the prayers were said.

The Weinsteins and some of the cast sang "Shalom Aleichem," which Mrs. Weinstein explained means "Peace Be Unto You," and after that Kurt's dad filled a silver cup with wine and recited the Kiddush. Finally, after lifting the challah bread in the air and reciting a blessing, he cut off a piece for everyone, explaining that the blade of the knife should always tip inward, toward the table, not outward, toward the guests.

Then we ate—roast chicken, gefilte fish, chicken soup, kugel. . . . There were more Sabbath prayers and hymns as the evening went on, ending with "Ein K'Elokenu"—"None Is Like Our Lord." As our parting gift to the Weinsteins, the cast sang one of the songs from *Fiddler,* the "Sabbath Prayer," and I had to blink and swallow, it was so moving.

The great-grandfather, in a voice we could hardly hear, said his Friday nights would never be the same after that. Neither would ours. Sharing the Sabbath with a family who truly understood the traditions would help us make *Fiddler on the Roof* all the more convincing.

• • •

The night of the first performance was gorgeous. Soft April-smelling breezes blew over the parking lot, and a half moon illuminated the cast members who ran into the building, holding their costumes over their arms, calling out to one another. The whole place was a buzz of excitement.

I loved the energy of it. Faith and I set about checking every prop to make sure it was in place—every chair, every pitcher, every bottle or basket or barrel just exactly where it was supposed to be, so there would be no surprises for the cast once the curtain rose. Molly and the guys were checking the lights, the microphones, the speakers—testing, retesting—and I fell right in beside them, helping out, forcing Richard to look at me so he could see I had survived my humiliation. I can't say he was exactly chummy, but that was okay with me.

The orchestra members were filing in, and now and then an instrument would tune up, then two or three at a time, making an awful racket. Faith and I peeked out from behind the curtain as the auditorium filled, families with young children in tow, parents carrying cameras for picture-taking afterward, friends of cast members coming in groups and sitting down near the front, everyone talking and calling out to one another, changing seats, long-legged guys stepping over the backs of one row to get to another.

Backstage, one of the girls had ripped her skirt, and Molly and I were desperately trying to find enough safety pins to make a new seam. Tevye had a headache, one of the cossacks had the flu, someone had taken the menorah off to be polished and it wasn't where it was supposed to be, one of the microphones was whistling, and Charlene Verona was being a pill. She had discovered herself. Again.

Just as Molly and I were trying to get our hands inside the skirt without making the girl take it off, Charlene appeared at our elbows, all aglow, and said, "Isn't mauve the perfect eye shadow for me?"

I looked at her and then at Molly as I took another safety pin from my mouth, but Molly couldn't help herself. "Charlene," she said, "did you ever hear of Galileo?"

Charlene looked at her nonplussed. "What?"

"How the earth's not the center of the universe?" Molly continued.

"Of course!" Charlene's brow wrinkled even more.

"Well, neither are you," said Molly. "We've got a hundred problems here. Be helpful. If you can't be helpful, could you at least be quiet?"

Charlene flounced off, but I don't think I could have said that in a million years. The menorah reappeared, polished, the skirt got pinned, somebody gave Tevye a Tylenol, an understudy took the cossack's part, and we all gathered in the wings.

"Break a leg," cast members whispered laughingly to one another—the good-luck blessing among actors.

I decided to focus my second article for *The Edge* on the tension backstage before the curtain rises—the assorted worries running through people's heads: *Are all the props in place? Do I need a cough drop? Is my fly zipped? Can I remember the words to the second verse?*

The orchestra director took his place in the pit and was going through the official tune-up now. It looked to us as though almost all the seats were filled. Then Harry got the signal to dim the house lights, the audience quieted down, and at last we heard the familiar strains of the lone violin.

The scene onstage was an open view of Tevye and Golde's hut, their yard to one side, and a backdrop of trees and other small huts in the village. There would be nine scene changes in act one and eight in act two, so the stage crew really had to hustle. When the lights onstage went off completely, we had to help the actors get to their places without falling over anything, so that when the lights came on again, there they were, the village was going about its business, and Tevye launched into the opening song, "Tradition."

When he sang "If I Were a Rich Man," the audience began clapping along to the rhythm halfway through, and that seemed to make him strut even more. I realized then how the audience takes part in a production—how they react to what's onstage and the cast responds to their reaction. I'd remember to put that in one of my articles. And when he ended at last on the phrase ". . . If I were a wealthy man," it brought down the house. Later, when the rousing "To Life" was sung by all the guys, the audience really got into it and clapped in time much of the way through. Backstage we all smiled at each other, relieved that it was going so well.

There were some glitches, of course, and we just hoped the audience didn't notice. A boy's beard came unglued and dangled off one side of his face, and another guy's pillow had slid so far down his abdomen, we were afraid it would slip out the bottom of his tunic.

"Grab that guy the minute he comes offstage and fix that pillow," Faith whispered to me, and I was able to get it tied in place again.

Tevye's daughters sang beautifully, even Charlene, I had to admit. We were eager to see how the audience would react to the ghost scene, where Lazar Wolf's dead wife supposedly speaks to Tevye in a dream. Some of the cast, dressed in white sheets, came moaning and keening down the aisle toward the stage while the ghost of the dead wife shrieked out her warning, seated high in the opening of the projection booth at the back.

The audience did just what we wanted them to do—turned and gasped—and that song got great applause, too. In all, the first night went off just as it should. Everyone whistled and clapped and cheered when it was over, loudest of all for Tevye, and after the cast took their bow, the stage crew were called out, so we linked hands and sort of line-danced our way across the stage in our black jeans and T-shirts, and then the orchestra took the applause and, last of all, the director. One performance down, three to go.

Dad and Lester came the second night. They were sitting in the second row off to one side. I was watching from behind the curtain when Tevye and Golde were singing "Sunrise, Sunset," and was surprised to see my father furtively wipe tears off his cheek. *Was he thinking about how he would feel when I married?* I wondered. Or was he thinking of Sylvia? Of Mom? I saw Eric there too, sitting on the other side of the auditorium, and he came around afterward long enough to tell me we'd done a good job on the scenery and props.

"You think you cccc-can squeeze me in some

w-w-weekend when this is over?" he asked.

I smiled. "I'll ask my secretary," I joked. "It can probably be arranged."

One of the cast members drove me home, and Dad and Lester were still up, making grilled cheese sandwiches.

"How did you like it?" I asked eagerly. "You had good seats."

"So close, we got spittle on us all through 'If I Were a Rich Man,'" Lester said.

"Orchestra was terrific, Al! And everyone sang with such enthusiasm. It was great!" Dad said.

"I especially liked the part where a stagehand came out to move a bench between scenes—one of the girls, I think, about your size, actually—and when she bent over we noticed a rip in her pants," said Lester.

"What?" I cried.

"Relax," said Dad. "It never happened."

I gave Lester a look, and after he went to bed I said, "Are you disappointed in me, Dad, because I can't sing? I really wish I could have been out there onstage, in the chorus, even."

"If you could carry a tune, you wouldn't be you now, would you? And I wouldn't change you for the world," he said.

How is it that fathers can word things exactly right?

"Well, I wouldn't change you for the world, either," I said, and gave him a hug. "Maybe in another life I'll come back as a canary. Or maybe I'll sing at the Met."

"I'll settle for whatever you do in this one," Dad said.

The whole gang came the fourth night of the production. Charlene, of course, went around backstage before the performance, hugging everyone, getting ready for her bawl when it was finally over, I guess. We noticed that friends of cast members in the audience came carrying single roses and bouquets to give to them afterward, and someone rushed backstage to say that all the programs were gone. We had a full house.

I suppose the final performance is always difficult because you know you're doing it for the last time. The audience was even more enthusiastic, and every actor seemed to be adding little flourishes to his performance. We were missing three understudies, including Charlene's—the flu was making the rounds—but the original cast onstage seemed healthy, and we had only this last night to finish.

During intermission, though, Charlene, in her usual "watch me" mode, was using backstage as a dance floor. Her face set in concentration as though she wasn't aware that Mr. Ellis was about and that people were watching her, she folded her arms across her chest and went whirling around and around, her full skirt twirling about her. Then, using every ballet step she knew, she went leaping from one end to the other, but when she turned to go back, she danced too close to a ladder lying on the floor and caught her foot behind a rung. She stumbled, twisting her leg, and fell to the floor.

I knew she had been trying to show Mr. Ellis that she could not only sing, she could dance. But I hadn't expected this!

She howled, and Ed and Devon ran to pick her up, but she was really in pain and somebody joked, "Hey, Charlene, when I said, 'Break a leg,' I didn't mean it!"

Mr. Ellis came over then and examined her ankle, which was beginning to swell.

"It's okay," Charlene kept saying, clenching her teeth. "I can go on, Mr. E."

But when she tried to stand up and put her weight on it, she couldn't. Suddenly Mr. Ellis grabbed my arm. "Alice, you're going to have to be Tzeitel in the second act," he said. "Charlene's understudy is sick."

"What?" I cried.

"You've got her hair, her build. You've been here enough, you know what to do."

"Mr. Ellis, I can't sing!" I croaked.

"You don't have to. She doesn't have any songs in the second act, and you can lip-synch along with the chorus. If you don't know what to do, fake it."

Charlene started to cry, and I almost cried with her. I had to admit that of everyone else on stage, I probably looked most like Charlene, and yes, I knew where she stood and what she did, which wasn't much in the second act. But . . .

There was no time for buts. We were already late with Act Two. Charlene cried all the while she took off her costume, and *really* sobbed as she handed it to me. I was numb with terror. One of her friends handed her a robe we kept backstage, and another located her parents in the audience. Ten minutes later, Charlene was on her way to Holy Cross Hospital, and I was tying her kerchief under my hair in back, and smoothing my apron over the long gingham skirt, wondering if I was going to throw up.

The guy who played Tevye came over and put one arm around me. "Don't worry," he said. "We'll guide you around the stage. Just act like you belong there and no one will know the difference."

I would swear that when the curtain rose for Act Two, I heard Pamela gasp, "That's *Alice!*"

I think I went through the whole second act in a trance. I could see the scenes in my mind, and could sort of place where Tzeitel stood, the few places where she had a line to say. Once, when I missed it, somebody else said it for me and it didn't really matter. I was never, ever, so glad to hear the final chorus, "Anatevka," and suddenly I began to feel loose and relaxed, and lip-synched my way through it as though I were singing my heart out. I could see Elizabeth and Pamela and Mark and Brian and Penny and Patrick staring at me in amazement from the fourth row. And then I realized that at least part of Lester's interpretation of my dream had come true: I *had* done something scary I'd never done before, but I didn't fall flat on my face.

To make the whole thing worse for Charlene, I got the bouquets intended for her, and when Tevye's three daughters held hands and came forward for their own special bow, my friends went crazy and cheered and clapped as though I'd been the star, which was almost embarrassing, but of course everyone else had friends there cheering for them, too. Molly and Faith grabbed me after the final curtain and gave me a hug. "You looked half scared to death, but with the villagers being scattered to the four winds, that was exactly right," Faith said, and we laughed.

When the gang gathered backstage, I had to explain how it had happened, and how I'd lip-synched along with the chorus, and then we went out into the hall where parents and friends were taking pictures and cast members were autographing programs. When people came up to me for my autograph, I had no choice but to write "Tzeitel" beside Charlene's name, and only one of them asked if I was the same girl who played it in Act One. Worse yet for Charlene, Sam was there taking pictures of the cast for the yearbook, and we all went back up onstage and posed for a couple of scenes. My name would appear under the stage crew listing, of course, but my picture would appear over Charlene's name.

Mr. E. said the stage crew would be expected to come back to school the next day and strike the set, but that we were all going to enjoy the cast party that night. I took off Charlene's costume because I wanted to go in my black jeans and T-shirt as part of the stage crew. We all piled in the cars of the juniors and seniors and drove to the home of the girl who played Golde, where her parents had prepared refreshments.

It was loud and noisy and fun, and there were a lot of silly awards given out—the person who came late to rehearsals most times, the person who took longest to learn his lines—and I was delighted to receive an award for "Most Grace Under Pressure," for filling in for Charlene. We laughed at all the things that had gone wrong, the last-minute changes the audience didn't know about, and then we presented Mr. E. with a miniature gold-plated fiddle that I had ordered specially through the Melody Inn.

It was one of the best times I'd ever had, and it wasn't until the end, when the cast sang "Sunrise, Sunset," as our final tribute to our director, that I realized Faith hadn't come to the party, and I would have bet my last dollar that it was Ron who had kept her away.

9

Clearing the Air

I woke up the next morning smiling at the mementos I saw strewn about my room: the black T-shirt with FIDDLER on the back. A bunch of flowers. A program. A poster. A black balloon from the party. I wandered around in my pajamas pinning things to my bulletin board, taping the poster to the wall. When I went down to breakfast, Lester had gone to play volleyball with some of his buddies, and Dad was looking up painters in the yellow pages because he wanted to have the inside of the house done before Sylvia came back in June.

"Have a nice time at the cast party?" he asked.

"Yes! I've made a whole new bunch of friends," I said. "A lot more people I can say hi to in the halls."

"It's nice to see you bloom, Al," Dad said.

"Huh?"

"Bloom. Blossom. Spread your wings."

Fathers are so strange sometimes. With Dad I'm either a flower or a bird.

"I'm going back to school today and help strike the set. I'll take the city bus," I told him.

"Okay, hon. It's just you and me for dinner tonight. Les will be out. Why don't we go somewhere? What appeals?"

"Let's try something we've never had before," I suggested.

"Okay. You pick the restaurant," said Dad.

When I got to the high school, most of the crew were there, and it was like another party, but less rowdy. Mr. E. had brought pizza and Cokes for us, and while the guys dismantled the sets, the girls were packing up props, sorting out things from the school's storeroom, boxing up the things we had borrowed from other people. Even Richard and Devon were more friendly toward me.

Mr. E. stayed until the backdrops were down and dismantled, and asked if we could finish on our own, which, of course, we could.

"Hey, Faith, missed you at the party," Harry called over. "You should have come."

"Yeah, I'm sorry I couldn't make it," Faith said, and sounded wistful.

"What could be more important than a cast party?" Molly called from the other side of the stage, where she was wrapping up electrical cord.

"Oh, Ron had other plans for us," she said.

Molly and I exchanged glances.

We were just finishing the last of the pizza and were going to stack the scenery and take all the stuff to the storage room when we saw Ron walk in through a side door. He stood for a minute with his hands in his pockets, a toothpick between his lips. One of the guys had been teasing Faith, making her laugh, and Ron didn't look too happy about that. He sauntered over, coming up behind Faith, and clapped one hand over her shoulder. "Hey, babe," he said. "Let's go."

Faith had just picked up a piece of pizza and opened a Coke. She turned around. "We've still got a lot of stuff to do," she said.

"Like what? Having a picnic? You said you'd be through by one."

"I know, but there's a lot of stuff that has to be packed up," Faith told him. By now, everyone had stopped talking and was watching the little drama.

"They can finish up. C'mon." We could see his fingers clamp more tightly on her shoulder.

"Let me eat this, then I will," said Faith.

"I'm parked in the custodian's place. C'mon," he said, and jiggled her shoulder so hard that the Coke spilled out of the can and onto her jeans.

I stared at Faith, at the way her face flushed.

She'd seemed to be having so much fun before.

Suddenly Harry stood up and took a step forward. "She said she wants to finish her lunch. Maybe you didn't hear," he told Ron. Ron looked up.

And then, to my surprise, Richard and Devon stood up, too. "This is a cast party," Devon said. "You can wait outside if you want."

"Hey, this is between Faith and me. It's none of your business," Ron said.

"Wrong, buddy. Faith's our friend, and you treating her like dirt is our business. She'll leave when she's good and ready. Right now, she's not ready," Harry said.

Ron's jaw clenched. He stared down at Faith. "You coming?"

She kept her eyes on her lap. "No."

"What?" said Ron, anger in his voice. "I didn't hear you."

"She said *no*," said Harry. "She's staying, and we'll see that she gets home."

Ron glared around the stage, then turned suddenly and left, and the rest of us broke into applause. I couldn't tell what Faith was feeling, embarrassment or relief or what.

"Good for you, Faith! You finally stood up for yourself," Molly told her.

I handed Faith a paper napkin to blot up the Coke on her jeans. "He's going to be really mad,"

I told her, wondering if we'd only made it harder for her. "He won't . . . he won't hurt you, will he?"

"Oh, gosh, no, he's just the jealous type. He means well."

"Wrong," said Harry. "He's a control freak, and you deserve better."

We awkwardly changed the subject then, as Faith silently finished her lunch. I didn't know if what had happened was enough to turn the tide or not. Maybe it meant a lot to her to have us all in her corner. Or maybe she just decided on her own that it was time. But as we finished packing up, I noticed that her color returned to normal, she was a little more talkative than usual, and Harry, true to his word, drove her home.

I was thinking about her on the bus later. Now that the production was over, it would be too easy to go back to our old clique again and forget about Faith. But this was when she needed new friends the most, yet I was afraid if I called her, she wouldn't want to do anything with me—a freshman trying to hang out with a junior. But I called her anyway when I got home and asked if she wanted to see a movie with Pamela and Elizabeth and me the next day.

"Thanks for asking, Alice, but I'm going somewhere with Molly," she said.

Well, that was good, too.

• • •

Charlene called me when I got home.

"It wasn't broken after all," she said. "Just a really bad sprain. How did it go, Alice?"

I knew that the only possible answer that would satisfy her would be to say that I fell on my face. "Well, I guess you'd have to ask someone else. I was too scared to think, almost," I said truthfully. "But the other kids covered for me. I don't think too many people noticed." She *definitely* did not want to hear that. "The show had to go on, and your understudy was sick. What else could we do?"

"They could have sat me in a chair or something," she said, and her nose sounded clogged, as though she'd been crying. "Mother was wondering if I got any flowers. I mean, I'm home now, of course, but I have to stay off my foot and wear this bandage, and . . . I *did* get flowers, didn't I?"

"We sort of divided them up among the whole cast and crew so that everyone got flowers," I said. "But I'll be glad to bring some over if you give me your address."

I called Elizabeth and Pamela and asked if they wanted to go on a mission of mercy.

"To where?" asked Pamela. "Who are we being merciful to?"

"Charlene Verona," I said.

"Are you nuts?"

"Probably. But she deserves her flowers. Les said he'd drive us over."

Liz and Pam have had a crush on Lester almost since the day we moved in, so they said they'd go. I'd just stuck the flowers I'd got at the performance in one of Lester's beer steins (*Remember to buy a vase before Sylvia comes to live with us,* I told myself), so I took some plastic wrap to wind around the stems and when Elizabeth and Pamela came over, we all crawled in the backseat of Lester's car.

"Dad and I are eating out tonight, Les," I said. "Where are you going?"

"Heavy date," he said as he backed out of the drive.

"Heavy as in fat?" asked Elizabeth.

"No. I'd say, maybe a hundred and thirty pounds, nicely stacked," he replied.

"Heavy as in *serious?*" asked Pamela.

"Heavy as in 'interest,'" said Lester. "Lauren's a very attractive, intelligent woman. Anything else you want to know?"

He left himself wide open on that one.

"Sure!" said Pamela. "How *intimate* are you with this woman, Les?"

"Pamela!" said Elizabeth, but I'll bet she was curious, too.

"Intimate as in 'soul mates'?" said Lester. "Intimate as in 'philosophically in tune'? Intimate as in—"

"Never mind," I said, knowing he'd never tell us, anyway. I checked the address Charlene had given me. "Turn right at the next light, Lester, then left at the second stop sign."

"So who is this woman, Lester? Your fave girl?" asked Elizabeth.

"Your latest conquest?" asked Pamela.

"Latest victim?" I put in.

"She happens to be one of my philosophy instructors at the U of Maryland," Lester told us.

"Isn't that against the law? Dating a student?" asked Elizabeth.

"She could go to jail for corrupting the morals of a minor," said Pamela.

"Ha!" I said.

Lester just smiled at us in the rearview mirror and pulled up to a gray brick house. "Here you are, ladies. Take your inquiring minds with you, please. How are you getting home, Al?"

"We'll catch a bus," I told him.

"Good-bye, sweetheart," said Pam, getting out.

"Have a good day, luv," said Elizabeth.

Charlene's mother met us at the door. She was a thin redhead who looked as though she could have been a dancer in her day.

"You're the girl who filled in for Charlene," she guessed when she saw the flowers. And when I nodded, she said, "She's in here," and led us to the living room, where Charlene sat with her foot propped on a hassock.

"Here are the flowers, Charlene," I said. "I'm sorry about your foot."

She hardly even looked at the flowers, just gave them to her mother to put in a vase. She seemed so much smaller—more vulnerable, maybe—hunched down in the chair in her pajamas. I was beginning to have mixed feelings about Charlene. She was pretty even in her pajamas with a bandage on her foot—naturally pretty. She'd been *born* pretty. And somehow I was holding that against her. That, and all her talent; she could sing like anything.

"So how did it go?" asked Mrs. Verona. "We went right to the emergency room and didn't get to see any of the second act. Such a disappointment! Charlene worked so hard!"

"Oh, it went great!" said Pamela. "Everyone said the final performance was the best!" I couldn't stop her. I wondered if Pam was jealous of her, too.

"But how did you manage?" her mother asked, turning to me. "Charlene said you can't even sing!"

Elizabeth answered. "I don't think anyone even knew there was a change," and Mrs. Verona looked stricken.

"At least you were there for the first act, and

that's the one that counted," I told Charlene quickly.

Mrs. Verona turned to her daughter: "Well, honey, it's only your freshman year. You have three more years to be in the productions. *I* wasn't in a musical till I was in *college!*" Then, to us, "Usually these roles go to the seniors. We were just so pleased to find out that Charlene got a major part. But she's so talented."

I started to say something nice, like, "Yes, she was very lucky," or something. After all, we *were* guests in their home. But Pamela piped up with, "Oh, and they took pictures for the yearbook afterward. Won't that be a hoot, Alice?"

"For the *yearbook?*" Charlene wailed.

"Don't worry. I gave your name, not mine," I assured her. "It's only fair that you get the credit."

"But it won't be Charlene's picture!" cried her mother. "I simply don't know why they had to wait till the final night to take pictures. I *so* wanted to have copies made and to send them out with our cards next Christmas! I had the whole thing planned, and now *this!*"

All the while her mother was talking, Charlene seemed to be sinking lower and lower in the chair, eyes on her mom, feeling worse, it seemed, that she'd let her down. I don't know if she'd leveled with her mother or not about how she had hurt her foot, but if I had a pushy mom like that, maybe I'd feel like whirling myself around and around—right off the end of the stage, in fact—anything to let off some steam.

"Well," I said quickly. "We just stopped in, Charlene. I really hope you'll be better soon. The kids'll fill you in on everything when you get back."

Her mother thanked us for coming over and took us to the door. We were never so glad to get out.

"Whew!" said Elizabeth.

"I guess it's hard not to think of yourself as the center of the universe if your mom believes that you are," I said.

"They make me sick," said Elizabeth. "Charlene with her perfect face, perfect skin, perfect everything. Her mother just wants her to be what *she* was. Or never was, one or the other."

"Charlene *did* look sort of pathetic," I said.

"You're *sorry* for her?" Pamela exclaimed. "Ha! It couldn't have happened to a better person. All she wants is to be the star."

That sure sounded familiar. We were jealous, all three of us! Pamela was accusing Charlene of wanting exactly the same thing she did. And wasn't it curious that Elizabeth, who had been fighting acne lately, happened to mention Charlene's perfect skin? As for me, hadn't I wished a few weeks ago that I could get up on a stage and belt out a song like the others did at the audition, Charlene included?

"Well," I said, "she *is* stuck on herself, and she *is* obnoxious at times, but if she were homely, we wouldn't be talking about her like this. Right?"

"If she were homely, she wouldn't be stuck on herself," said Pamela.

But Elizabeth can see a moral a mile away, and you can make her feel guilty about almost anything. Maybe jealousy is a sin. "So we can dislike her for being conceited, but we can't dislike her for being pretty and talented and loved and coddled?" she said.

I nudged her in the ribs. "Hey, Elizabeth, *you're* pretty and talented and loved and coddled, and we don't hate *you!*" I grinned.

She just elbowed me back.

"Listen," I said. "Dad and I are going out for dinner tonight. Someplace we've never been before. You guys want to come?" I knew he wouldn't mind.

"Sure," said Elizabeth.

"If it's okay with him," said Pamela.

We went to an Afghanistan restaurant and had little deep-fried *sambosas* for an appetizer, and *quabill palow* for the main course—lamb and saffron rice with carrots and almonds and raisins. And somehow, after a great dinner in good company, we began to feel that we could make it through three more years of high school with Charlene Verona if we really worked at it.

My last article for *The Edge* was about the production as a community—the actors, the orchestra, the director, all the different stage crews—and how it takes all of us to bring a musical to life. All of us deserve the applause. I described the cast party afterward, how we'd been through something big together, and felt sort of like family.

Nick and Sara said it was the best writing I'd done so far, and that made me feel really good. Things were suddenly going well for me again—I'd made new friends, was back on track with my old ones, Patrick and I were pals, Gwen was helping me with algebra when I needed it, I was fine, Dad and Sylvia were fine. Lester and Lauren were . . .

"So how was *your* evening?" I asked Lester at breakfast the next morning as I buttered my English muffin.

"Well, I'm seeing her again next weekend, if that answers your question," said Les, who doesn't usually care much for early morning conversation.

"You're getting an A in her course, I presume?" I chirped.

"My course work and our relationship have nothing to do with each other," said Les. "There's no law against an instructor and a student having intellectual discussions and enjoying cultural events together. This is college, after all, not high school."

"Be careful, Les," said Dad.

On Monday, in the middle of the morning, I got a pain. It was somewhere down around my navel, but I started getting these sharp little stabbing pains that turned into a steady throb by lunch-time. I wasn't sure if I was going to throw up or not, so I didn't eat anything.

"What's the matter?" asked Gwen.

"I don't know. I've got this pain in my abdomen."

"Cramps?"

"No. I had my period just a week ago."

"Then it's probably not ovulation, either," said Gwen.

"Ovulation gives you a bellyache?"

"Sometimes—when the egg breaks out of the ovary. Does it feel like a stomachache?"

"Not exactly. Just sort of a throbbing, burning pain."

"You ought to go see the nurse—have it checked out," she said.

I made a little face. "Probably something I ate," I said.

"I don't think so," she said. "You didn't eat any-thing for lunch, right?"

By fourth period, the pain was unmistakably worse. I asked for a pass and went to see the nurse. She asked me the same things about my period and had me lie down on the cot. Then she bent over me and gently prodded my abdomen. When she got about halfway between my navel and my hipbone on the right side, I gave a yelp.

She put a thermometer in my mouth, and when she came back and checked it, she said, "I'm no doctor, Alice, but my guess is you've got appen-dicitis. I think we ought to call your dad."

"Is that—?"

"It's not serious, but I rather think you're going to have your appendix taken out."

"An operation?" I gasped. And the next thing I knew, I felt the room going around, and I blacked out.

10

The Girl in White

When I came to, I heard the nurse talking on the phone to my dad. She must have been sitting beside my cot, stroking the side of my face with one hand and holding the phone to her ear with the other.

"Alice? Alice?" she said as I struggled to open my eyes. And then, to my dad, "She's coming to now, Mr. McKinley. She's going to be fine. . . . Yes, I'll tell her you're on your way."

I felt as though I were down in a deep, deep well. I could hear what was going on and feel the nurse's fingers on my cheek, but I didn't have the energy even to open my eyes.

The nurse grasped my fingers. "Alice," she said, "if you can hear me, squeeze my hand."

Somehow I managed to do that, and then I opened my eyes.

"I think that was a bit of a shock, and I could be

completely wrong about that pain in your tummy, but if I'm not, it's about the most common operation you could imagine. It's really not a big deal," she said.

I just looked at her. It was *my* abdomen we were talking about, not hers.

"Your dad's on his way over, so you just lie there and rest a little," she said.

I didn't say anything because I was afraid if I opened my mouth, I might vomit.

A girl came in with a sore throat, and a guy who had hurt his thumb in gym. They could probably see my legs and feet sticking out from behind the curtain, I realized, and I turned my face toward the wall.

The pain was pretty constant now. It throbbed like a finger when you get a cut on it. Finally I heard my dad's voice out in the hall, then coming through the door, and next, right beside me.

"Al, honey?" he said. "Think you can sit up?"

Wincing, I sat up and he crouched down beside me. I put my arms around his neck and started to cry. "I don't *want* an operation!" I sobbed.

He stroked my back. "Now let's don't jump to conclusions. Dr. Beverly said he'd see you as soon as I brought you in, so let's let him have a look at you." He reached down to get my shoes off the floor and helped put them on my feet.

"She has a temperature of a hundred and one,"

the nurse said. "And the pain's definitely in the right place."

"Thanks for taking care of her," Dad said. And then, to me, "My car's right outside. Just take it slow and easy."

Of course the bell had to ring just as we moved out into the hall, and as kids passed, staring at Dad with his arm around me and the way I was walking, sort of bent over and holding my stomach, they parted to make room for us, and I felt like Moses parting the waters of the Red Sea.

Eric passed us, then suddenly jerked around and stared at me. "Alice?" he said.

"Hi, Eric," I said, but some kids pushed between us just then, and Dad and I turned and went out the door.

I cried all the way to Dr. Beverly's. "I don't *want* an operation," I wept again. "I don't want an ugly scar on my belly. I want to wear a bikini, and I'm *scared!*"

"Al, there are a lot worse things than a scar on your abdomen."

I knew there were, but I didn't want to hear about them.

Dr. Beverly took me right in when we got there, and it was a good thing, because I threw up in his wastebasket.

"Oh!" he said, and rang for the nurse, who wiped my face and left with the wastebasket. Then I promptly threw up on the floor.

I figured the nurse would come in this time with a mop. She did, but she also gave me a basin to hold on my lap, and just staring down into it, knowing what it was for, made me upchuck again.

Dr. Beverly wanted to know which came first, the pain or the nausea. The fever or the tenderness in the abdomen. This time when I was being examined, I shrank away when he got even close to the place where it hurt. He took my temperature again, and this time it had gone up half a degree.

"Appendicitis," he told Dad. He made a few calls, then told Dad to take me over to Suburban Hospital in Bethesda, that the surgeon on call said he could take me within the hour.

By now the pain was relentless, and I didn't think about the operation much, I just wanted the pain to stop. Dad got me admitted to Suburban and waited outside my room while the attendant helped me get my clothes off and put on a hideous white cotton robe that tied in the back. Then she rolled me over onto a stretcher. Dad sat with me while I waited to go to the operating room. He held my hand and patted my shoulder till they wheeled me in.

I hated the strangeness of the operating room. The big metal mirror and the instruments and lights. The surgeon came in and had to poke me again just to make sure I'd yell, I guess. I started crying.

"What if I d-don't wake up?" I mewed.

Dr. Salinas smiled. "Well, I've only done about a hundred and sixty of these, and I've never failed to have one wake up yet," he said. He bent over me.

"Wait!" I gasped. "What if I wake up too soon while you're still operating?"

"Won't happen," he said. "I guarantee it."

A nurse moved in. "Wait!" I cried. "What if . . . what if you leave something in me before you sew me up?" I thought of all the cartoons I'd seen of doctors leaving sponges and things in patients. "What if you leave a pair of scissors?"

"That won't happen, either," he said, his eyes smiling above his mask. "We need every pair of scissors we can get."

Why hadn't they put my robe on with the opening in front? I wondered. Now they would have to roll me over and untie the robe and roll me back again.

"Wait!" I cried as the nurse put something in my arm. I wanted to explain about the fading tattoo on my bottom but then I felt myself beginning to sink deliciously into sleep, the noises around me grew fainter, and I felt my arms relax.

I couldn't tell how long I had been out. My first thought was that I must have fainted again, and as my eyelids fluttered, I saw that I was in a bed with metal sides.

"Al?" came Dad's voice. "You're doing fine, honey."

I think I drifted off again. Then Lester's voice: "We could always fill a bedpan and dump it on her."

I opened my eyes and saw him standing over me.

"Don't . . . you . . . dare," I managed to say.

He grinned. "She's awake."

"How do you feel, sweetheart?" asked Dad, and I realized he was standing on the other side of me.

I felt my tummy. There was a bandage. "Is it over?" I asked, surprised.

"All done. You came through with flying colors."

The nurse walked in. "Well, look who's awake," she said, and adjusted something in my arm, then cranked the head of my bed up a little.

I realized I was feeling quite good, actually. Sort of foggy and fuzzy. My belly was sore, but the throbbing pain was gone.

When the nurse had checked on me and taken Dad out in the hall to direct him to a rest room, Lester handed me something wrapped in tinfoil and tied with string. "A little present," he said.

I slowly untied the ribbon. Everything about me seemed to function in slow motion. My fingers felt all thumbs. Inside the foil wrap was a small jar, and inside the jar . . . I couldn't figure out what it was.

"Appendix," said Lester. "The surgeon thought you'd want to keep it."

"Oh, gross!" I said, looking at it curiously. About the size of a pinkie, it was thin and white and shriveled, sort of lumpy at one end. "What am I supposed to do with *this*, Les?"

He shrugged. "Wear it on a chain around your neck, give it to an admirer, feed it to a pet . . . I don't know."

I went home the next day. Dad took off work to take care of me until he was sure I could manage on my own. I was still a little wobbly, and had to keep the bandage dry, but by the day after that I was perfectly able to be by myself, and the doctor said I could go back to school the following Monday, but couldn't take gym for a while. Dad sort of let me take over the living room and gave me all kinds of little projects to do to keep me occupied and to help us get ready for Sylvia—a box of unmatched socks to sort through; the same with a box of shoelaces; pictures to put in albums; clothes to be mended . . .

Pamela and Elizabeth came to see me, of course; Karen dropped by with Gwen, and a lot of people called.

"Oh, my gosh, was it awful?" Pamela asked. "Alice, you're the first one of us who ever had an operation."

"You don't feel a thing," I told her.

"Do you have to be completely naked?" Elizabeth wondered.

"I have no idea. I was unconscious, you know."

"If I ever have an operation, I'll have a local anesthetic," Elizabeth declared. "I want to know absolutely everything that's going on.

It was when I was checking my E-mail later that I found a note from Eric.

> Hey, what happened? Someone said you
> were sick.
> CAY

I E-mailed back:

> Just a little appendicitis, is all. I'll be
> back in school on Monday.

It was time, I decided, that Eric meet the rest of my friends. So when I got a second message from him, *Can I come over? Sunday afternoon, maybe?* I E-mailed back, *Sure,* and invited Pamela and Elizabeth and Mark and Brian and whoever else wanted to come, too. I said we'd have a nachos party, and I put on my soulful, sick-little-girl look for Lester. It actually worked. He went out and brought home a large order of nachos and some

sodas, which was a good thing because Karen and
Jill and Justin showed up, too, and later, Patrick. I
was wearing my best sweats and just socks on my
feet, and felt perfectly comfortable.

Eric was surprised to find a room full of people
when he came to the door, but I grasped his arm and
pulled him inside. "Eric, you probably know most
of these people," I said. "Eric Fielding, everybody."

Patrick had been telling a story of something
that had happened on the last band trip out of
town, and we were all listening to that, so it gave
Eric a chance to settle down in a corner with a
plate of nachos, and he's most relaxed when he's
not the center of attention.

"So three guys sneaked out to bring back some
beer, and the rest of us locked the door on them,"
Patrick said.

"Where were you, a motel?" asked Mark.

"No, a dorm, in Towson. They'd really been a
pain, spouting off the whole trip about how, when
we got to Towson, they were going to do this and
they were going to do that, but we had a big competition coming up the next morning. So after
they left we locked our room door, and evidently
the custodian locked the front door, too. When
they got back with four six-packs, they couldn't
get in, and they didn't know what room we were
in, what window was ours."

We all started to laugh.

Patrick was laughing, too. "So they decided to hide the beer first, then figure out how to wake us up, then come back and get the booze. They made two mistakes: They threw gravel at a window and it happened to be the band director's, and later, when they went down to get the beer, after he'd let them in, the unlocked car they'd put it in had driven away."

We hooted.

"Eric, are you in the band?" asked Mark.

Everyone turned to Eric.

"N-N-No," Eric said, his face coloring a little.

Brian grinned. "I take it that's a n-n-no?"

All faces turned from Eric to Brian. I couldn't believe he'd said something so insensitive.

"Brian!" Elizabeth murmured disapprovingly.

But Eric, strangely, smiled, too. "Y-Y-Yes," he said, smiling, and this time it seemed he was stuttering on purpose. "That was a n-n-no."

We all laughed then, and I thought how well he'd handled it.

"Eric's on the track team with me," Patrick explained.

"We t-teamed up in the rrr-relays," said Eric.

"Came in second, too!" said Patrick.

The gang stayed for a couple of hours. Of course, we had to pass around the jar with my appendix in it.

"Oh, get it *out* of here!" said Karen.

"It looks like a finger," said Jill.

"A uvula," said Gwen.

"A what?"

"That little thing that hangs down the back of your throat between your tonsils," she said.

Mark studied the jar. "Looks more like a part of the private anatomy of a male monkey," he said, and we all laughed. I had to be careful of my stitches when I laughed.

Patrick, however, held the jar in his hands, turning it this way and that, and finally he said, "You know what this is, Alice? A piece of white asparagus."

"What?" I said.

He unscrewed the lid and sniffed. "Preserved in vinegar," he told us.

"*What?*" I shrieked again. Then, "Lester!" as I caught sight of him out in the hall.

He poked his head in the doorway. "You called?"

"That's not my appendix, it's asparagus," I said.

"Is that a fact?" He grinned. "Well, you can't blame me for trying. I was in the Safeway and wondered what I could pick up for you. Balloons and flowers cost too much, but the produce man let me have a stalk of white asparagus for nothing, slightly wilted at the ends. But with a little imagination you can see it's a decaying remnant of the large intestine, a little gangrenous there in the middle with. . . . Say. Anyone got an appetite for more nachos?"

When everyone left about four, Eric stayed a while longer. He looked around at all my half-finished projects for Dad and picked up the box of assorted shoelaces. "Starting a c-cottage indus-try?" he joked.

"Dad's put me to work cleaning out drawers and stuff, getting ready for his wedding this summer," I said, and told him the story of Miss Summers and how they'd met at the Messiah Sing-along.

All the while I was talking, I noticed that Eric was playing around with the shoelaces, and then I realized he wasn't exactly playing, he was idly tying intricate knots. "What are you, a sailor?" I asked, and he grinned.

"N-Not exactly. I was a SSSS-Scout once, and had to learn a zillion knots," he said.

I went over and sat beside him, and he showed me how to tie a figure eight, a fisherman's knot, a stopper knot . . .

"Congratulations," he said. "Remind me to send you my camping badge when I get home."

The phone rang. It was Pamela.

"I'll call you later," I said. "Eric's here."

"He's still there? Oh, definitely! Call me back!" she said.

Eric and I talked about movies and favorite vacations and sharks and what food we would miss most if we were stranded on a desert island. Eric said what he would really miss was his CD player, and then we talked about our favorite songs and I told him how much I liked the music from *Fiddler on the Roof.*

"I liked those articles you wrote for *The Edge,*" he said. "Especially the one about how you felt watching the others s-sing, and you can't carry a t-tune."

"Yeah," I said. "It always looks so *easy* for them. How do they *know* they're singing the right notes? I've always wondered, and Dad says they can just hear it. Well, I can 'hear' myself, of course, but I can't tell if I'm on the right note or not. It seems so magical to me, that others just *know.*"

Eric smiled ruefully. "That's how I feel," he said. "T-Talking always looks so easy for everyone else."

"Just to open your mouth and say the words?" I asked.

"Yeah. Instead of all this sss-stopping and ssss-starting."

"And practice doesn't help?"

He laughed. "I can ssss-stand up on a stage in an empty auditorium and recite the P-Pledge of

Allegiance without a hitch, b-but let one p-person come in, and I ssss-start ssss-stuttering again. I discovered that from experience."

"Then it doesn't sound like something you were b-born with," I said, and suddenly stared at him. "I just stuttered!"

He laughed. "So it's catching!" Then he put two fingers under my chin, turned my head toward him, and kissed me.

I liked being surprised that way; I didn't have to worry about it in advance. I blinked and just looked up at him when he let me go. And then he kissed me again.

We both smiled at each other afterward. So I laughed and said, "What was the second kiss for?"

"For k-keeping your mouth shut after the first one," he said.

I leaned back against his arm. "Well, if you don't practice not stuttering, what does your therapist have you do?" I asked.

"More s-stuttering."

"What?"

"He says the more I c-can do it openly and easily, the m-more I'll relax. And when I don't try so hard to fight it, I won't k-keep my tongue or my jaw or throat muscles so tense. And everyone else will feel more comfortable, too."

I sighed. "I wish it was the same for singing. No

matter *how* relaxed I am, nobody wants to listen. I was practically banned from singing 'Happy Birthday' at parties when I was little."

Eric laughed out loud.

"In fact, when I was in grade school, and all the other kids were singing, the teacher gave me the triangle to play instead."

We both laughed that time. Eric kissed me again. "I like you b-better with your mouth closed," he said.

"See?" I told him. "Even *you* think so!"

When I called Pamela later, she asked, "How long did he stay?"

"I don't know. Another hour, anyway."

"He really *is* crazy about you, Alice!"

"Well, that's nice to know," I said.

"So, what are you going to do?"

"What do you mean?"

"I mean, he likes you, but he's a stutterer!"

"No, he's a guy who happens to stutter, along with a whole lot of other stuff he does very well, Pamela."

"Like what?"

"Like kissing," I told her, and we laughed.

11

The Color Purple

Lester was in love.

Again.

Well, he didn't use the word "love," and he said it was an intense, intellectual relationship, but I know Lester, and he was more nuts over this woman than he'd been over someone in a long time. I figured any woman was better than his last girlfriend, Eva, a walking clothes hanger, who criticized everything he did. Several nights a week at the dinner table, Les told us about his conversations with Lauren that he said were helping to sharpen his mind.

"So what did we learn at school today?" I asked him brightly over the chili.

"Actually," said Lester, spearing a piece of broccoli, "we're comparing John Stuart Mills's distinction between higher and lower pleasures with Aristotle's Nicomachean Ethics."

I was sorry I'd asked; what I really wanted to

know was what Lauren had said to him before or after class and what he'd said to Lauren. "What about lunch?" I asked. "Did you eat with her again?"

"Usually she eats in the faculty dining room, but sometimes I can persuade her to eat with me out on the grass, if the weather's nice. That's where we have our best discussions. Mills's approach, see, is that some pleasures are different and superior to others, and he chooses the higher pleasures, those of the mind versus those of the body."

"And you're for the pleasures of the body, of course," I said.

"Well, that's what we're discussing. Mills says that anyone who says the lower pleasures are better isn't qualified to judge, that you need to be trained and educated to appreciate the higher things. And while there may be some truth to that, I say that maybe the intellectual has lost the capacity to enjoy some of the lower pleasures."

"All work and no play makes Jack a dull boy?" I said helpfully, trying to condense the argument.

"You might say that, yes!" Lester said, and looked at me appreciatively as though I had actually said something important.

"And Lauren's view?" asked Dad.

"Well, right now we're discussing the fact that not *all* intellectuals have lost the capacity to enjoy the lower pleasures."

"You, for one," I said.

"Darned right." Lester sprinkled cheese over his chili and took another bite.

"These discussions over lunch," said Dad. "I assume that anyone can join in? Anyone passing by you out on the grass?"

Lester shrugged and thought about it a minute. "I suppose. We don't exactly put out a welcome sign, but if anyone came along and wanted to join in, we wouldn't stop them. We're just so intent on the conversation, we don't like to be disturbed."

Dad didn't say anything more. If anybody was disturbed, I'd say it was Dad.

Les and Lauren may have been intellectual buddies, but the fact that he wanted to bring her by the house to meet us obviously meant something, so I put on my best jeans and a clean shirt to look halfway decent.

My scar had almost healed—it hardly showed—and I was able to take gym again. I was so happy to be back in the World of Well that I felt I was ready for anything. Operations don't sound like much when they happen to someone else, but when they happen to you, when it's *your* mind that's going to sleep, and *your* body that's going to be cut open, it's not so casual anymore.

I ran the sweeper over the carpet and wiped out

the bathroom sink. I also made a pitcher of iced tea and a quick-mix coffee cake. About four o'clock the following Sunday, Les pulled up in front of the house, came around to the passenger side, and opened the door for a brown-haired woman in a blue short-sleeved sweater and slacks, wearing tiny pearl earrings and a floating pearl necklace. She was about the same height as Lester, with a small waist and broad hips—nice looking— more handsome, I'd say, than beautiful.

Lester gallantly held one hand under her elbow as he guided her up the steps.

"Lauren, this is Alice, and my dad, Ben," he said, and we politely shook hands all around before we moved into the living room and I set about slicing the cake.

She had an interesting-looking face, but I think she was a little uneasy with us. There was a sort of forced self-confidence about her that made her begin each sentence louder than it ended up, as though she was trying to convince herself that she was still the instructor here, oblivious of the lovesick puppy look on Lester's face.

"How are you liking the University of Maryland?" Dad asked her, handing her a glass of iced tea.

"Well, I got my degree from Ohio State," she said, "and Maryland seems a bit more personal, more manageable. This is my first teaching job, and I was very lucky to get it, even though it's just adjunct instructor."

"She got the job because she's smart, period," Les said proudly.

Lauren gave him a fond, admonishing look. "And Les is one of my best students. He's the only graduate student taking my course, actually, but he needs it for his degree."

The coffee cake was pretty awful. I thought maybe I had taken it out of the oven too soon, because the center was gummy, and we all sort of ate around it, mauling our slices just enough to show we'd tried.

"Is the pay comparable with other universities?" Dad asked.

"I suppose so," said Lauren. "It's not a lot, but"—she stopped and smiled at Lester—"Les has been so good at showing me around—the least expensive restaurants, all the things there are to do on campus. He's been a great guide."

Obviously. Les never seemed to be home anymore. He was on campus every night. There, I'd guess, or Lauren's apartment, and I suspected the apartment.

She was originally from Tennessee, Lauren said, and Dad told her he was from Tennessee, too. They talked about Nashville and Memphis, while I poured more iced tea for everyone and had to keep running to the bathroom. I threw out the rest of the cake.

Nothing Lauren said indicated that Lester was more than a friend to her. But once, when I came back in the living room and Dad was out in the kitchen getting more ice, I noticed that Les was rubbing his thumb over her hand.

Eric invited me to a coffeehouse one evening. It was held in a church basement, where small tables had been set up with red-and-white-checked tablecloths, and a candle in the middle of each. Eric said there would be music and poetry and stuff.

"Are you going to read something?" I asked.

"No. Just listen over a c-cappuccino," he said.

Probably most of the people there were high-school seniors or college age, but we seemed to fit right in. I guess the coffeehouse was run by a singles group at the church, who served as waiters, and I ordered a mocha, which arrived under a heap of whipped cream and a cinnamon stick.

"So is this where you hang out?" I asked him.

"N-Not exactly," he said.

"But do you come here a lot?"

"Not exactly," Eric said, smiling.

I gave him a quizzical look. "Have you *ever* been here before?" I asked curiously.

"Nope," he said, and we both laughed. "I just w-wanted sssss-something different."

The first person to read was a man with a beard who read several far-out poems in a sort of dry, distant voice, and twice Eric rolled his eyes at me, asking if I wanted to leave, I guess. But after that a girl stood up and read a funny monologue about some of her fantasies when she rides the Metro. Then a guy played the guitar and sang, and by the end of the evening, though I could hear liquid sloshing around in my stomach whenever I changed position, we decided it had been fun.

.Eric walked me home—all fourteen blocks— because it was a gorgeous spring night. We held hands, and I was thinking I could really get to like this guy, if only he were sticking around.

"Your moving to Dallas is definite then?" I asked.

"'Fraid so."

"Do you have any brothers or sisters? How do they feel about it?"

"A mm-married sister in Missouri, so it d-doesn't affect her."

"What does your mom think?"

"She's all fff-for it, because that's where she's from. We've g-got relatives all over T-Texas."

"Oh. So it's not like you're moving to a distant land or anything."

"N-No. In fact, I've g-got a ccccc-cousin who says she's going to ggg-give me a pppp-party when I get there. She sss-says I'll have girls swarming all over me."

I laughed. "Lucky you," I said.

"Lucky me," said Eric. Then he said, "I'd g-give it all to be with you."

"Ah!" I said. "What a great line, Eric! It sounds like the last line of a poem."

"Hmmm," said Eric, starting to smile as we walked along. Then he began, "'I wandered lonely as a cloud . . .'"

"'When all at once I saw a crowd . . .'" I put in, teasing, realizing that his class must be studying Wordsworth, too.

"No, no, that's the third line," Eric said. "It's 'That floats on high o'er vales and hills . . .'" He nodded at me to join in then, and we both said together, "'When all at once I saw a crowd, A host of golden daffodils.'"

Eric was grinning now. "Though Dallas beauties do await . . ."

I made up the next line: "Um . . . beneath a sky of azure blue . . ." We were really into it now, and I discovered that he didn't stutter when he was reciting something.

"And rosy lips shall be my fate . . . ," said Eric.

Together we ended with, "I'd give it all to be with you."

We gave each other a high five.

"Hey, we're really good!" I crowed. "Do you think we should read it at the coffeehouse sometime?" We both laughed. "I didn't know you liked poetry," I told him.

"I d-don't, exactly. Well, that's not true. Mom always read t-to us, so I like it, but I go mmm-more for the adventurous poems—'The Cremation of Sam Magee' and stuff."

I let my head rest on his shoulder. "Tonight was a lot of fun, Eric," I said. "I'm going to miss you."

He looked down at me. "There's E-mail, rrrr-remember?"

"Yes," I said. "How could I forget?"

We stopped and kissed then, a long, long kiss that would have been embarrassing it was so long if I'd thought he didn't mean it. It wasn't like Patrick's kisses. Eric's were a little more intense, maybe—sort of a signature kiss, all his own.

If I felt bad that Eric was leaving, the one thing I felt good about was that I didn't see Faith and Ron together anymore. They ate at separate tables in the cafeteria, and though I couldn't say that Faith looked happy, at least she wasn't being ordered around by "The Corporal," as we called Ron.

Pamela and Elizabeth had gone to the auditorium over lunch one day to watch a fashion show put on by the home arts department, but I slipped outdoors to enjoy ten minutes of spring sunshine, and found Faith sitting on the school steps, hugging her knees, her eyes closed, face tilted toward the sun.

I sat down beside her. "You, too?" I said.

She opened her eyes. "Yeah. It feels *so* good. I'm always cold."

"Maybe you should take up basketball—get the blood circulating," I said. She didn't answer, so I added, "How are things?"

"Between Ron and me?" she asked.

"Well, that, too."

"I hear he's not dating anyone," she said.

"Surprise, surprise!" I said. "After the way he treated you, who would have him?"

"You only saw one side of him, Alice. I saw his tender side. Some guys hide part of themselves when they're around other people, you know? But when it was just the two of us, he was so incredibly loving."

I didn't know what to say. Finally I asked, "Did you ever wonder, though, why he felt the need to treat you like that in public?"

"Yes." She laughed a little. "It was just his defense. He's really an old softie inside."

"But . . . doesn't it bother you that he had to be so controlling, Faith? I mean, it was as though he didn't want you to have any friends except him."

"It's just that he needed me so much, Alice." She shrugged. "And sometimes it's nice to be needed."

"Oh, Faith, you've got so much going for you! You've got a whole lifetime ahead of you and . . ." I sounded like Aunt Sally.

"I know, I know. I'm just reliving old memories. Just a slight case of sunstroke, that's all," she said.

"I would hope so," I told her, and laughed.

The most difficult part of my freshman year was not the course work (except for algebra) or finding my way around, it was juggling all the different parts of my life. And I didn't even have a boyfriend. Not officially, anyway. Eric may have been seeing other girls, for all I knew, and he never asked if I was seeing anyone else. We didn't go out every weekend or anything like that, and he never called. We were just friends. Erotically charged friends, I suppose Les would say.

It helped that *Fiddler on the Roof* was over, but there was still my work on the newspaper, my assignments, my Saturday job at the Melody Inn, my friends and family, the housework. I was very careful to do something each week with Elizabeth and Pamela, but Dad seemed to be asking me to do more and more around the house to get it ready for Sylvia, and there just weren't enough hours in the day to do everything.

I was complaining about it to Marilyn at work one Saturday. "I'm only one person!" I cried. "I have only two arms and two legs."

Marilyn was sorting though mail orders to see which had been filled and which were still waiting for supplies to come in. "Doesn't Les help out?" she asked.

"He's so crazy over this new girlfriend that he—" I stopped.

"It's okay, Alice," she said.

But I knew it wasn't okay. It would never be okay as far as Marilyn was concerned, because I didn't think she'd ever gotten over him.

"So tell me about her. What's she like? I promise not to cry," she said.

"She's a new philosophy instructor at the U, and I don't think Dad's too happy about it."

"If she's faculty, then she should know better than to date a student," Marilyn said.

"I guess there's no reasoning with a woman in love," I said. I paused, realizing suddenly that Marilyn did *not* look especially sad, did *not* have tears in her eyes. In fact, she was taking it very well. "So what's new with you?" I asked.

"I'm dating again," she said.

"The trombone teacher?" I said, thinking of all

the men who gave music lessons in the practice cubicles upstairs.

"No. He's a guitarist who plays with a group in Baltimore. A friend introduced us."

"That's great!" I said. "How long have you been seeing him?"

"About a month now."

"No wonder you look so sparkly!" I told her, and she laughed.

Dad had gotten up early Sunday morning to make waffles, and left the batter for Les and me. I was making a second waffle when he stumbled into the kitchen in his T-shirt and boxer shorts. It was one of the pairs we'd given him for his birthday, with a lipstick pattern all over it, red ruby lips half parted for a sensuous kiss.

"You want this waffle?" I asked. "If you want it, it's yours."

"Never look a gift horse in the mouth," said Les. "Sure."

"What does a horse have to do with anything?" I asked.

"Never mind," said Les. He poured himself some coffee and sat down at the table.

I slid the waffle toward him, then the butter and syrup, and sat down across the table. I knew he and Lauren had gone to a concert the evening before. "Have a good time last night?" I asked.

"The best."

"Good concert?"

"Passable. But the company was excellent." Lauren, he meant.

There was something about the satisfied look on his face that made me study him a little more intently, and then I saw a large hickey mark on the side of his neck. That *really* made me worry. Just how intimate were they? I wondered. What if he got Lauren pregnant? What if she lost her job? What if Lester suddenly found himself a husband and father and he wasn't even through grad school yet? What if he grew to resent her and reject the baby, and Dad and Sylvia and I would have to take the baby in, and I'd be the aunt who raised this little child who . . . ?

"Lester, you *are* using birth control, aren't you?" I gasped.

The fork fell out of his hand. "What?"

"You're so in love with her, and—"

"Al, can it! I'm more than seven years older than you, and I don't ask if *you* use birth control, do I?"

"I don't."

"What?" he said again. "Meaning . . . ?"

Dad came back in the kitchen to refill his coffee cup. "What are we talking about?" he asked.

"I'm not sure," said Lester.

"Birth control," I said.

"*What?*" cried Dad.

"What" was the favorite word at breakfast that morning, it seemed.

"If Les and Lauren aren't using any kind of birth control, Dad, I think we ought to decide right now if we can accept the responsibility of a little baby in our house while Lester finishes school so he won't abandon his wife and child," I said.

"*What?*" yelled Lester. "I thought we were talking about you, Al."

Dad's head swiveled from one of us to the other. He decided to focus on me. Almost in a panic, he said, "If you're thinking of having sex at the age of fourteen, Al, forget it. But if you decide to have sex, anyway, I hope you will go to Dr. Beverly and discuss it confidentially."

"None of the above," I said. "It's Les I'm worried about."

"Well, then, I wish you'd stop," said Lester. "Lauren and I are both adults, and I can handle myself just fine."

"I hope you're right," Dad said, and had to sit down right then to get his bearings.

Elizabeth was having another fight with her folks. She called and asked if she could spend the night, and I told her to come over in about an hour.

Gwen was there helping me with algebra, and I couldn't take on Elizabeth's problems until I'd solved my own.

Gwen had told me once she wanted to be a singer. "You should be a teacher," I said. "I can't make sense of algebra in class, but when you explain it, I can catch on enough to squeak by."

"Lack of self-confidence, girl. That's your problem," she said.

"Huh-uh. Lack of intelligence."

"What's with Elizabeth?"

"She's coming over to spend the night. Problems with her folks again."

"Looks like you're running some kind of shelter here," Gwen said, smiling.

"For wayward girls," I told her. "You want to stay?"

"Can't. Told my grandfather I'd be home in time to play him a game of cards," she said, and grinned.

What I couldn't figure was that Elizabeth got mad at her parents over every little thing these days. She'd been in therapy now for about four or five months, and though I think she was feeling better about herself, her parents were feeling worse. I could see that she might be mad at them for not having suspected that their friend had been molesting her when she was younger, but it seemed as though she was going to hold it against them forever. I even began to wonder if she hadn't already worked this through and was just using it as an excuse to rebel against any other thing she didn't like about them. Elizabeth had been such a dutiful daughter for so long that, now that she'd had a taste of what it felt like to rebel, she couldn't get enough of it, it seemed. Pamela and Gwen and I just wondered how far she'd go.

"Elizabeth's coming over to spend the night," I told Dad. "And she's upset."

"Man the lifeboats," said Lester.

"Do her parents know she'll be here?" Dad asked, not wanting a replay of what had happened last summer when Pamela once spent the night.

"They know," I said. "At this point they're probably glad to get rid of her."

I was at least half right, because Elizabeth walked in dressed in purple from head to toe. She had tinted her hair purple, was wearing purple eye shadow, mascara, lipstick, and nail polish, and had on a long, granny-style purple dress with a purple stole.

Now what? I wondered.

Once in my room, she whirled around and faced me. "I *like* it, okay?" she snapped.

"Did I say anything?" I asked. "You can paint your behind purple for all I care, Liz. Don't jump on me!"

"Sorry." She dropped her bag on the floor and stood with her arms folded, staring out the window. "No matter what I do, they're against it!" she complained. "Every little thing."

I smiled a little and studied her some more. "Sure you're not just trying to get a rise out of them?"

"I *like* purple!"

"So, fine! You look good in it! Just come up for air occasionally, will you?"

"You know what, Alice? I don't know who I am," she said ruefully.

"You're Elizabeth," I told her. "Take a seat and stay awhile."

"Hey, Al!" said Lester. "You've got a birthday coming up. The big ol' one five!"

"Yeah?" I said. "What's the proper gift for a fifteenth birthday, Lester? Rubies? Emeralds? Sapphires?"

"Plastic," said Les.

"Les-ter!"

"No, seriously. I thought of something else. I told Lauren I wanted to do something special for your birthday, and she suggested taking you to a show in Baltimore—a play, actually—a spoof on Italian weddings called *Tony 'n' Tina's Wedding.*"

"Oh, Les! Really? I've heard kids talk about it."

"You seemed to have such a good time with *Fiddler on the Roof.* I could get tickets for us next Friday night, the day before your birthday. They were sold out on Saturday."

I threw my arms around him. Going somewhere with Les was always special. Then I wondered if I had to share him with Lauren.

"Is Lauren coming, too?" I asked.

"No, she has something else going on."

Good! I thought. "How should I dress?"

"Like you're going to a wedding, I suppose. The audience is part of it, I think."

I wish he'd said I could bring some friends, but knowing how expensive tickets were these days, I knew he was already spending far over his budget.

"We could go Dutch," I said. "I've got some money saved."

"Hey, kiddo. It's your birthday. It's on me," he said. "Just don't do anything to embarrass me, okay?"

12

Tony and Tina

Aunt Sally and Uncle Milt had sent me a check for my birthday, and I splurged on a dress I really loved. Marilyn went with me on a lunch hour at the Melody Inn to buy it. It looked sort of like a slip—just a short, backless, cream-colored sheath that covered the front of me, but was completely bare in back from the waist up except for the halter strap around the neck and two thin strings that tied below it.

I giggled when I saw myself in the mirror. So did Marilyn.

"Lester will have a spaz," she said, "but it's good for his heart. He needs to exercise it a bit." We giggled some more.

"Now shoes," said Marilyn. "You need something light."

"I have a pair of beige flats with thin cross-straps over the top," I told her.

"Perfect," she said.

"But what do I do for a bra?" I wondered, checking the dress again.

Marilyn put her hand to my ear. "You don't wear one," she said.

"But . . . my *nipples!*"

"So you have two little points down there. It's not against the law."

"But, Dad—"

"I know. Better not let your dad see you in it at all."

"Oh, Marilyn, I love this dress, but do you think I should?" I asked her.

"Be adventurous," she said. "And blame it on me."

Fortunately, the night we were to go to *Tony 'n' Tina's Wedding,* Dad was going to a chamber music concert with the clarinet instructor from the store and his wife, and they left before we did. I waited till he was out the door and down the drive before I put on my new dress and came downstairs, where Lester, in his good sport coat and pants, was reading the paper.

"I'm ready," I said.

"Good for you! Right on time," he said, looking at his watch. "Never keep a date waiting if you can help it." He looked me over. "Nice dress."

"Thank you," I said.

"Except for your . . . uh . . . mammary glands,"

he said. "Can't you sort of walk round-shouldered so they're not so prominent?"

"Don't be ridiculous, Les," I said, and started for the door.

"Al!" he gasped. "You're naked back there!"

I tried not to laugh. "I am not. There are strings—"

"What if some guy reached out and pulled them?"

"They'd untie, I suppose," I said. "But there's still the halter strap."

"But . . . there's nothing at the sides! A guy could slip his hand in there!"

"Not with you here to protect me," I said. "You sound like Aunt Sally, Lester. Don't tell me you wouldn't be delighted if Lauren wore a dress like this."

"You're not Lauren, Al. You're fourteen years old."

"Fifteen tomorrow," I said.

"In that dress, you're jailbait."

I just smiled sweetly. "Shall we go?"

One of the things I like about my brother is that when he offers to take me some place, he treats me like a grown-up. He's not patronizing, doesn't act as though he can't wait for the evening to be over. It *was* my birthday present, after all.

So we headed toward the beltway and the road that would take us to Baltimore, and I had to keep reminding myself that I was dressed. I'll admit, though, I felt as naked as Lester thought I looked. I wasn't used to feeling the back of the car seat against my bare shoulder blades, but I looked, well, *sexy* in front, the shape of my thighs under the thin fabric of my dress, no slip underneath.

"Am I dressed appropriately for the occasion, Les?" I asked. "I mean, do I look as though I'm going to a wedding?"

"No, you look as though you're going to work in a strip joint."

"Les-ter!"

"A *nice* strip joint, I mean."

"*Les*-ter!"

"A really classy dump."

"Lester, I don't care what you say, I am going to Tony and Tina's wedding in this dress and I think I look ravishing."

"So you do. That's why I worry."

Lester pulled up to the address that was on our tickets, and after we'd parked, we went inside and up the stairs, where a crowd of people were milling about a lobby outside a makeshift chapel. Immediately a grandmotherly looking woman in a navy blue dress came up to me and said, "It's been ages! Oh, you look so good, and you should see Tina! She's absolutely beautiful."

While I was still staring, an elderly man grabbed Lester by the arm and kept shaking his hand up and down, saying, "So glad you could come! So glad! I've got another grandchild since I saw you last. Look here at little Anna." And he pulled out a worn plastic picture folder with photos of people we had never seen before, and I guess we were supposed to play along, because Les said, "And look at little Teddy there. He's the spittin' image of you, Gramps!" The man laughed and slapped Les on the shoulder, and ambled off to show his pictures to someone else. I grinned at Lester, and he grinned back. This was going to be fun.

"You want a 7UP or something?" he asked.

"Sure."

We had to stop by a desk to turn in our tickets and were given our table number for the reception. The woman sitting there was obviously doubling as a bridesmaid. Two men in tuxedos were arguing loudly nearby as to which one had dated the bride most recently, and everyone was watching and laughing. It was as though we were all onstage, and none of us knew our lines, but it didn't really matter. We were just part of the chorus. As long as I didn't have to sing, I didn't really care *what* happened.

While Les was at the bar getting my soft drink, a third man in a tuxedo sidled up to me and said how much he liked my dress. "An extraordinary dress," he said, examining it from all angles.

Les moved in. "Excuse me, she's with me," he said.

The tuxedoed man put up his hands. "Hey, hey! No offense! Just looking, no touching."

Then a large guy wearing shades, who looked like a member of the Mafia, stepped up on a chair and bellowed, "Okay now, all youse who came to celebrate the marriage of my buddy Tony to his dame shoulda got your table assignments by now, and you can put your drinks down where you can find 'em later and go in the chapel there. No fair takin' somebody else's drink when you come out, either, you're too cheap to buy your own."

We laughed and headed toward a door with fake stained glass, and found ourselves in a small chapel with flowers in front. Les and I sat down next to the aisle because I wanted to see the bride when she came in. The old grandfather was the first relative to come in, though, and he was still stopping along the aisle to show off pictures of his grandchildren. Then the father of the groom came in with his new trophy wife in a very low-cut red dress with black fishnet stockings, and finally the mother of the bride, who had greeted us when we first arrived.

The recorded organ music began, and an actor in priest's robes stood up in front along with a nun who was supposed to be a relative of the bride.

It was a funny ceremony, with the grandfather having to go to the bathroom in the middle of it, the nun leading the congregation in a rousing hymn she'd written herself, then the wedding procession, with one of the bridesmaids obviously pregnant and chewing gum.

Tony, the groom, was too laid back to suit the priest, and Tina, a beautiful actress, was annoyed with him because he kept forgetting what to do. But at last they were "married," and we all went to a large room for the reception and dinner.

Les and I were seated at a table where we could see both the wedding party at their table and the dance floor, and there was something going on every minute. Having taken part in the school production, I could appreciate all that the actors and actresses had to do, because they had to improvise a lot, and they doubled as waiters and waitresses, wheeling out the steam tables, dishing up the food, and organizing the buffet line.

We never knew what was going to happen next because the actors kept mixing with the audience, coming by and pretending they knew everyone, as though we were all relatives. Of course one of the bridesmaids got a little "drunk," and somebody's aunt "fainted." Tony and Tina themselves got into an argument because she thought he had insulted her mother, but toasts were made, then there was dancing, and when one of the ushers invited me out on the dance floor, Les just smiled and shrugged. "Enjoy," he said.

While we were dancing, though, the actor kept peering around at the back of my dress, making the audience laugh, and then he began fumbling with the strings as though he was going to untie them. Tina, who was dancing with her "father," reached over and slapped his hands, and everyone laughed again, including me. When he took me back to our table, Les grinned, and I admitted I'd actually enjoyed being out there on the dance floor, like I was one of the performers myself. It was fun going along with the act.

Then the father of the groom insulted the mother of the bride, the father's new wife climbed up on a table and began dancing, the nun kept trying to lead the audience in song, and the tipsy bridesmaid came over to our table and invited Les to dance. "C'mon, honey," she said. "I've had my eye on you all evening."

Wanting to be a good sport, he got up and escorted her out on the floor with some other couples.

For the first few minutes they danced like everyone else, the tipsy bridesmaid smiling at him and flirting. Les rolled his eyes at me as they waltzed by our table, and I laughed. But then the bridesmaid began leaning more and more heavily against Les, as though she were barely able to stand up straight, and he struggled more and more to hold her up. She put her head on his shoulder, one arm draped around his neck, and when they danced by a second time, I saw that her other hand was clutching the seat of his pants.

There were a lot of other crazy things going on around the room, but the people in the audience who were sitting nearest me saw the little drama going on between Lester and the bridesmaid. More and more people began watching, laughing and pointing, and I could tell that the bridesmaid was not about to stop and let him go. In fact, two of her fingers were drumming a tattoo on Lester's behind while she scrunched up his pants even tighter.

For one of the few times I could remember, I saw Lester blush. His neck, his cheeks, his forehead were pink, and he was good-naturedly trying to extricate himself from the woman, but she wasn't about to let him go. The more he tried to edge her back to a table, the more she clung to him, and Lester, his face really red now, resigned, kept on gallantly moving her around the floor while she played with his bottom.

I don't know how I had the nerve—emboldened maybe by being Charlene's substitute in *Fiddler,* or the fact that the audience was supposed to play along with the story, or maybe because I knew that no matter how outrageously I behaved, I'd never see any of these people again. But I suddenly got up from the table and, taking my 7UP glass with me to look more sophisticated—it was in a wine goblet—I edged out onto the dance floor and over to Lester and the bridesmaid. I couldn't tell if Les was more relieved or alarmed, but I tapped the bridesmaid on her broad back and said, "Excuse me, I'm cutting in."

I saw some of the other actors glance around, amused.

The bridesmaid never got out of character for a moment. She opened one eye to look at me sideways and, in a slurred voice, said, "Yeah? You and who else?"

"You're dancing with my fiancé," I told her.

"Well, sweetie, I think your fi-an-say fancies *me,* if I say so myself," she said, and plunked her head on Lester's shoulder again.

I was really in the spirit of things now, and everyone was looking at us and smiling. It was all a big joke, I knew, and they were playing for laughs, but there was a slight edge of anger roiling up inside me, too. I had to save my brother!

I tapped her again. "I want him back," I said.

She kept her head next to his, her lips an inch away from his face, and said, "She wants you back. Imagine that. Well, she can't have you, luv, 'cause you're mine. Allllll mine!"

Les was beet red now.

She turned her body so that she and Les were dancing away from me. I simply held out my hand and poured my 7UP right down her back.

Everyone gasped, but the other actors and actresses were laughing, and a couple of them even applauded.

The bridesmaid instantly let go of Les and stared at me. And then, actress that she was—and mindful that I was a paying customer—said, "Well, don't have a hissy fit, sweetheart. He's all yours!" and she huffily left the floor, the large dark stain spreading out over the back of her dress.

I set my empty glass on the nearest table, smiled sweetly at Lester, and put one hand on his shoulder as he danced me around the floor. Everyone was smiling at us.

"Hey, babe, I didn't know you had it in you," he said, looking slightly stunned.

"Neither did I," I said, and gazed at him with fake adoration. It was so much fun. Everyone figured we were a couple. So this was what it felt like to be one of Lester's girlfriends, I thought; this was the way it was for Crystal and Marilyn and Eva when they danced with him. For Lauren, too, maybe. Except they were in love with him, and I simply loved him as a brother.

I lifted my head and looked into his eyes again. "Les, do you remember the time you took me out to a club on my thirteenth birthday and while you were in the rest room this guy came on to me, and you rescued me?"

"Yeah. How could I forget?"

"So now we're even," I said.

"Thanks," said Lester.

The bridesmaid came back with a big towel stuffed down the back of her dress, and that made it all the funnier. Every time she passed our table she hissed at me and gave me dirty looks, but I could tell she was enjoying herself as much as anyone.

I guess when you put on the same play night after night, you hope something spontaneous will happen to liven things up. You want the audience to react and keep you going—anything to help your performance.

As soon as the wedding cake was cut and served, Les said. "You ready to call it a night, Al? Should we duck out?"

"I'm ready," I told him. "We've got to drive back to Silver Spring." We moved over to the door where some of the wedding party were saying good-bye to guests. The bridesmaid was at the end of the line, and when I got to her, she smiled and gave me a quick kiss on the cheek. "No hard feelings, luv," she said, and gave me the rose in her hair as a memento. As we started up the stairs, however, she reached out and gave Lester a pinch on the behind.

I'd forgotten that Dad would be home before we would, but when I saw him, I burst into the living room, full of our evening, wanting to tell him everything.

"Al!" he said, before I'd got a whole sentence out. "Where's your dress?" I looked down quickly, afraid it had somehow fallen off. "What?"

"Uh . . . that *is* her dress," Lester said, throwing his suit coat over the back of a chair.

Dad was horrified. "It's just a slip!"

I decided I might as well get this over with, so I struck a modeling pose and turned slowly around.

For a moment, Dad was speechless. He stared first at me, then at Lester. "You let her *go* like that?"

"Well, Pops, she *is* fifteen. And I was along to see that nothing happened."

"And you're going to go along every time she wears that dress?" Dad asked.

"Dad, backless dresses are *in* now! You should

see what the prom dresses look like this year!" I told him.

Dad leaned back against the sofa and shook his head. "I don't think I'm ready for this, Al," he said.

"Marilyn thought I looked great in it, and so did . . ." I started to say "all the men at *Tony 'n' Tina's Wedding*" but I knew that would send Dad over the edge. "So did Lester," I finished.

"Well, it is a nice-looking dress," Lester admitted.

"Come here," Dad said to me, and when I walked over, he sat me on one knee. I laughed.

"I can remember," he said, "when you were only a year old, in a little pink playsuit, and I'd bounce you on my foot."

"I don't remember that at all," I said.

"Of course. You were too young. And when you were three . . . four . . . wearing your OshKosh overalls, you'd sit in my lap and snuggle back against me while I read *Goodnight, Moon* or *Little Bear's Visit*. And now here you are, almost all grown up, attracting the glances of admiring men. . . ." He smiled at me and patted my hand. "I wish I could put you in a protective bubble, hon, and keep you safe forever, but I know I can't."

"She'd miss all the fun," said Lester.

"I know," said Dad.

"I'd never meet anybody," I told him.

"I know," said Dad.

"I'd probably grow up to be neurotic as anything."

"I know," Dad said again.

"And I'd never marry or get a job, and I'd be on your and Lester's hands for the rest of my life," I added, leaning over to kiss his forehead.

"Whoa! No plastic bubble for her, Dad!" cried Lester. "Zip, zero, zed!"

13

The Instructor Flap

Elizabeth and Pamela had already given me earrings for my birthday, and Eric sent balloons, but the next day, my official birthday, Dad gave me time off from the Melody Inn to go to the movies with Molly—her present to me. We'd gotten there early and bought a large tub of popcorn to share between us. I told her about *Tony 'n' Tina's Wedding,* and how I'd had to rescue Lester.

"I wish I'd been there to see that," Molly said. "You just reached out and poured your drink down her dress?"

"It was all I could think of to do." I giggled. "She wasn't about to let go, and she looked like she was trying to give Les a wedgie." We laughed some more. "What's surprising to me is that I actually enjoyed myself, everyone looking at me. I didn't think I'd have the nerve."

"I *know* I wouldn't!" Molly said.

"Maybe I'll try out for the senior play when the time comes," I said. "I probably wouldn't get a part, but—"

"Nothing ventured, nothing gained," Molly finished for me.

We heard a familiar voice several rows back.

"I thought you said 'buttered,'" came a girl's voice.

Then a guy's: "I said *un*buttered. Salt, no butter."

"So?"

"So go get me salt, no butter."

"Oh, Ron—"

We turned to see Faith getting up, setting the unwanted popcorn on her seat and heading up the aisle again as Ron put his feet on the back of the seat in front of him. Incredibly, he took a big handful of the popcorn he'd said he didn't want.

Molly and I stared at each other. "She went *back* to him?" I said in disbelief.

"Looks that way."

"Why?"

"A glutton for punishment, I guess," said Molly.

After the movie we went to the rest room and Faith was there, waiting in line.

"Faith, what happened? I thought you broke up with Ron," I said. Tactful, that's me.

She shrugged self-consciously and gave a little

laugh. "Who can explain love?" she said, and ducked into a cubicle.

Molly and I went to a Starbucks afterward and sat at a little table, still musing about Faith.

"That's not love, that's an addiction," Molly said.

"That's why I want to be a psychologist," I said. "I want to know why. No, I want to stop it before it begins."

"Good luck," said Molly.

When I got home, a small, flat package was waiting for me from Sylvia. I opened it and found the framed photo of her and me that was taken at White Flint Mall over spring vacation. I had sort of a weird smile on my face in the picture, but it wasn't bad. It looked like a mother and daughter having lunch together, and I wondered if I really would get used to calling her Mom.

Of course I had to call Elizabeth and Pamela and tell them about *Tony 'n' Tina's Wedding,* and they laughed at the way the bridesmaid had danced with Lester.

"The next time we come over, we each should pinch him on the buns," said Pamela. "I'd do it just to see Lester blush."

"Well, it takes a lot to embarrass Lester," I told her.

We call May the Mad Month at school because it's so frantic. There's statewide testing, for one, and all big assignments are due. The seniors who have applied for colleges know where they've been accepted, and while they might feel they can slide through till graduation, the freshmen and sophomores and juniors aren't so lucky.

Eric and I went for ice cream after lunch one day, and sauntered back to school, cones in hand.

"I ggg-guess we're g-going to b-b-be moving n-next m-month," Eric said, and I'd never heard him stutter so much in one sentence. But he didn't seem at all upset by it.

"Does your dad have a house already?" I asked.

"Yeah. It's about the ssss-size of the one we've gggg-got nnnn-now." He was smiling at me.

I smiled back quizzically. "You aren't doing that on purpose, are you?"

"D-Doing w-what? M-Moving?"

"Stuttering."

He laughed. "You guessed."

"Why?"

"It's an assignment. D-Desensitizing myself, so I won't freak out when I sss-stutter. I'll get so used to doing it in public, I won't fight it."

"I don't know anything about stuttering," I said, "but that makes sense. The more you try to keep from doing something, the more scared you are it'll happen."

"I'm learning to just let it c-come," he said.

"Okay b-by m-me," I said, and we laughed.

• • •

Dad and I were sharing a supper of baked beans and corn bread and tomatoes when he said, "You know, Al, if you want to work full time at the store this summer, we can use you, but I don't know if this is good for you or not."

"What do you mean?"

"Well, it's the same thing you've been doing, working for your dad. You're not getting out and exploring the world."

"I'm not exactly climbing Mount Everest, no," I said. "But if you'd like to send me to Paris . . ."

"I thought what might be an ideal arrangement would be for you to work for me part of the summer, but take a few weeks, at least, to do something else."

"Dad who's going to hire me for only a few weeks?"

He handed me the Style section of the *Washington Post,* where he'd checkmarked an article on summer camps for children and, in a side column, a few camps that ran for only a few weeks and needed assistant counselors, fourteen years of age or older.

I tried to think about what Dad was really saying. It was true I wasn't getting a lot of experience just working for him all summer. But I wondered if part of it wasn't his need to be alone more with Sylvia before the wedding—just have her here getting

used to our house, making suggestions for redeco-
rating, cooking together, all the little domestic
things they'd be doing after they were married—
without me around putting in my two cents' worth.

"I'll think about it," I told him.

I called Gwen to see if she was interested, and
she said maybe. I called Elizabeth. "I'd be willing,"
she said. "Let's do an overnight camp if we can get
it. Mom and I need to be apart for a while before
we kill each other."

I would never in a million years have believed
that Elizabeth would say something like that; she
was always so close to her mom. But maybe the
fact that she could bring out negative feelings like
this, even jokingly, was a good sign. Maybe she'd
just never felt before that she could.

I called Pam next, and she said almost the same
thing. "Dad got a letter from Mom. She wants to
come back," she said.

"What?"

"She walked out on the NordicTrack instructor
and moved in with another guy, and he left her,
and now she wants to come home. Dad says no
way. If she does come back and they start fighting
again, I'm going to move out, I swear it. See if you
can get a camp that runs all summer, Alice."

You know what's weird? Life. All these years, it
seems, I've been looking for a mom, and now that

I'm about to get one, I'm planning on going away. And Pamela and Elizabeth, who've had one all their lives, want nothing more than to get away from theirs. Once Dad and Sylvia marry, though, I think she'll be the kind of mom I want to be around always. She's never been a mother, of course, but she's been a teacher, and it can't be that much different, can it?

I called all the camps listed in the *Post* to find out more about them. The only one that sounded just about right was Camp Overlook, near Cumberland, Maryland: three weeks, from June 18 to July 10. The director said she'd need to interview all four of us, but she was impressed when I told her that Gwen and I had volunteered last summer to work in a hospital, and that Elizabeth and Pamela and I had spent some of spring vacation reading to kids at the Martin Luther King Library.

When the forms came, we each filled one out. Had we ever been arrested for driving while intoxicated? Had we ever used illegal drugs? Had we ever been arrested for abusing children? Shoplifting? I wondered if they were going to take our fingerprints, too.

The last day of school, when classes were officially over, we went to the interview together in Rockville. Pamela's dad drove us over, and Lester said he'd pick us up.

Our interview was in the county office building, and Camp Overlook, we found out, was run by the county specifically for underprivileged children in foster homes.

Miss Martinez looked us in the eye. "You're going to get a lot of sad-faced youngsters in need of far more than what three weeks at camp could possibly give them. Some will come with a chip on their shoulder, angry at life and angry at you, and all of them come with a certain amount of emotional baggage. The most we can hope for in that short a time is to give them a respite from the kinds of lives they've lived and get them to smile. We're not miracle workers, though we do see miracles now and then."

I think all four of us were wondering if we could do this, but Miss Martinez looked thoughtful. "These kids are all going to come back to the very same problems they've had before, but perhaps a little better equipped to deal with them. We do try to set aside some time each day for our counselors to unwind and socialize with one another, but basically you will be on call twenty-four hours a day. A kid may need you in the middle of the night. He may be scared or angry or confused or sick or homesick or all of the above. Many of them have never even been in the woods before, or seen a lake. This is your chance to make a difference, even a small one. If you don't think you can take their constant need for attention, then this job isn't for you."

She smiled at us and waited. "There's no disgrace in saying you can't handle it, you know. But we'd rather find out now than after you get there. Your room and meals, of course, are free."

Elizabeth and Pamela and Gwen and I sat mutely mulling it over.

"I think I can do it," said Gwen.

"It doesn't sound easy, but I want to try," said Elizabeth.

"Me too," said Pamela, and I nodded.

"Okay," Miss Martinez said. "If you change your minds, please don't wait till the last minute to tell me. You'll each be getting more information in the mail about what to bring with you, and it will tell you a lot more about the camp. Any other questions?" We shook hands as though we were mature adult women, and felt very grown up as we sat out on the steps waiting for Lester.

"What I *really* wanted to ask was whether any guys had signed up for assistant counselors, but I was afraid I'd jinx my application," said Pamela.

"Do you think we can really stand three weeks of constant 'neediness'?" I asked.

"It'll give me a break from being on call at home," Gwen smiled. "There's always an aunt or a grandmother wanting something."

Elizabeth said, "I asked myself if I could stand a whole cabin full of kids acting like Nathan at his crankiest, but these are older kids, six to ten, so I think I can deal with that. At least they can say what's wrong, not just fuss."

Lester drove up and my three friends piled in back. I sat up front with him. "Home, James!" I said grandly.

"So? How did it go?" he asked.

"We're hired!" Elizabeth said. "You'll be rid of us for three whole weeks this summer, Lester. What will you do without us?"

"Celebrate," he said.

We all trooped inside for a while, eager to talk about what we'd take to camp. Les said he was going upstairs to study, could we please keep our shouts and groans and giggles to sixty decibels?

"Sure, Les," Pamela said and, as he started up the steps, she reached out and pinched his buns.

After dinner that night, Lester got a phone call from Lauren. He answered on the phone in the downstairs hall but, after talking a few minutes, he said to me as I passed, "Al, I'm going to take this call upstairs. Would you hang up down here?"

"Sure," I said.

I held the phone to my ear while Les went upstairs. When I heard him pick up, I lowered the phone, but not before I'd heard him say, "Lauren, there's got to be a way around this."

I put the handset back in the cradle and wondered what he was talking about. Then I sat on the couch waiting for him to come back down. My first thought, of course, was that Lauren was pregnant, except I wasn't at all sure they'd been sleeping together. Or maybe she belonged to a strict religion and wasn't supposed to marry outside the faith. Or maybe she was taking a job in Alaska.

Dad was trying out some new sheet music at the piano, and then he just set it aside and played one of his favorite Beethoven sonatas, one that Sylvia especially liked, and smiled as he played.

I didn't want to ruin the piece, but as soon as he finished, I asked, "What's going on with Les and Lauren?"

Dad shrugged. "Is something going on?"

"That was Lauren on the phone. They've been talking for twenty-five minutes."

"You've been known to go for an hour or more," he said.

"I know, but he seemed so serious."

"Well, if he wants to tell us, he will," Dad said.

The phone rang again around nine, Jill wanting to know about an assignment. I realized then that Les and Lauren's conversation was over, but he hadn't come back downstairs.

When he hadn't come down by eleven, though, I went on up, washed my face, and put on my pajamas. When I came out of the bathroom, I saw that Lester's door was open and his room was empty. Then I heard him and Dad talking down in the kitchen.

I knew I shouldn't eavesdrop. In fact, I felt sure now that Les had been waiting for me to go to bed so he could talk to Dad. But I felt I had to know. If my brother was in trouble, it was my business, too, wasn't it? I was part of the family, too.

I made my way downstairs one step at a time until I could hear most of what they said.

"I hate to say I told you so, Les, but I think you knew this was a possibility," Dad was saying.

"I know, I know. I just didn't think they'd come down on her so hard. She's certainly allowed to have friends. I think she's overreacting to a few remarks people may have made. She admits that no one came right out and said she couldn't go on seeing me. . . ."

"What's at stake here is her impartiality, Les," said Dad. "She wasn't just dating a student, she was dating one of *her* students. You've been getting excellent grades in her class—deserved, I've no doubt—but it would be hard to prove that she wasn't favoring you."

"But we could still see each other off campus! I don't have any more courses with her, so how could it hurt? Why do we have to break it off completely?"

So that was it! For only the second time in his life, maybe, Les had been dumped. There was a quiver in his voice, and it always scares me when Dad or Lester is in pain.

"Maybe she was just plain scared and wants to rectify a foolish mistake. She'd undoubtedly like to become a professor, and doesn't want to jeopardize that," said Dad.

"But if I could just talk with her face-to-face . . . ! We . . . we love each other, Dad."

There was silence in the kitchen. Finally Dad said, "Are you sure of that now?"

"Well, I love her, and I thought . . . You think she's using this as an excuse to break up with me? Is that it?"

"I don't know. All I'm saying is that if she sees a way around it and wants to renew the relationship, I'm sure she'll let you know. Maybe she needs time to think it over."

There was real anguish in Lester's voice now, and I could hardly bear listening to him: "I can't just let her go! She owes me a better explanation than this!"

Dad's voice rose. "Les, be reasonable. I know this hurts, but she owes you nothing. She was new in town, you were a ready and willing guide—a friend—and I'm sure she valued your friendship. But is it possible you read more into the relationship than what was there?"

"Don't tell *me* what was in our relationship and what wasn't! What do *you* know about it!" Les snapped.

"I don't, although—"

"Well, then, butt out, Dad! You don't know anything about it; we were a lot closer than you think."

"In that case, this relationship can only lead to more trouble for her, Les, and if you care for her, you won't put her in harm's way," Dad shot back.

I wanted so much to go down and put my arms around Lester, but I went back up the stairs, instead, and into his room. I left a note on his pillow.

Luv you, Les.
Me

It wasn't the same, I knew, and it wouldn't help much, but there are times I think people need every little bit of love they can get.

14

Changes

I guess if I had to sum up my freshman year in one word, it would be "changes." I came out of my shell and got "involved," as Pamela was always telling me to do, while Pam and Liz sort of took a time-out. I made new friends and almost lost Elizabeth and Pamela because of it, and Les, in a strange turn of events, got dropped by a girl instead of being the dropper. It seemed as though the only person whose life wasn't on a roller coaster was Dad, and if anybody deserved some happiness, Dad was the one.

Frankly, I couldn't understand why Les and Lauren couldn't at least date over the summer, and hang out where no one could see them. But Lauren would be teaching some summer courses, and Les would be on campus taking a course, so it would still be a faculty-student no-no, and Les was taking it hard.

The first day of summer vacation, I gave myself the pleasure of eating breakfast in my pajamas. Les was already up, getting ready for his part-time job in a shoe store. He wasn't eating his usual bagel, though, just staring down into his coffee cup. Dad had already left for the Melody Inn.

I thought of how often Lester had been there for me when I'd had problems, and wished I could do the same for him.

"Les, I'm really sorry about you and Lauren," I said, opening a new box of Wheat Chex and pouring some into a bowl.

"So what do you know about it?" he rasped.

"I happened to hear you and Dad talking last night."

"'Happened' to, my eye. You were eavesdropping."

"Well, I'm worried about you," I said. "Do you want to talk about it?"

"No."

I got milk from the fridge, poured it over my cereal, and started to eat. After a minute or two, when Les still didn't speak, I said, "Am I chewing too loud for you?"

"Yeah. I can hear you breathing, too. Stop chewing and breathing and I'll be fine." He took another sip of coffee and stared morosely out the window.

"The course of true love never did run smooth," I said helpfully.

Les didn't answer. When that didn't seem to help, I said, "Every cloud has a silver lining, Les." And when he still didn't say anything, I said, "Whenever a door closes, you know, a window opens."

"Will you stifle it, please?" he growled. "What are you? The Book of Proverbs?"

"I'm just trying to make you feel better, after all the times you've been there for me."

That seemed to soften him a little. He got up and refilled his cup, then stood leaning against the counter, still staring out the window.

"I just thought we had a good thing going," he said at last. "I was even starting to feel I might have found the right woman for me and then, just like that, I get the brush-off."

"Yeah, she was about a thousand times better than Eva," I said.

"That's for sure," said Les.

"Maybe she'll teach at another college here, and then you can date all you want," I said.

"I don't think so," Lester said. "She's hoping she'll be hired again next year, and if she's asked, she won't have much use for me."

I hated to see my brother look so sad. There *had* to be a way around it if they were really in love, regardless of what Dad said.

"Then what you've got to do, Les, is have a

secret courtship until *you've* got *your* Ph.D., and then you won't be a student anymore."

"A three-year secret courtship?" he sneered.

"If she's the love of your life, it's worth it," I said.

"So what do you suggest, doctor? She has Caller ID and doesn't answer my phone calls. She won't answer my E-mails, either. Maybe she thinks they've got her place bugged, I don't know."

"You've just got to do something wild and reckless, Lester! She still sees you as a student. Be a take-charge man! Do something so romantic, so full of animal magnetism that she can't resist."

"Like what? Grab her by the hair as she comes out of the faculty dining room and drag her off to my den?"

"No, but if you were to climb through her window at night with a bouquet of flowers or something—oh, Les, she'd just melt in your arms."

Lester was looking at me strangely, and I realized I had his attention.

"Where does she live, Lester?"

"An apartment off-campus."

"What floor?"

"It's a garden apartment. Ground floor."

"Perfect! It's destiny, Lester! You'd knock her socks off if you showed you cared that much about her."

Les continued staring at me for another fifteen seconds. Then he put his cup down. "You're nuts, Al," he said, and left the kitchen.

A few days later, Eric came over and we went for a long walk, holding hands like Patrick and I used to do. In fact, I found us walking around the same block, down the same sidewalks that Patrick and I had walked the night we broke up. Were these streets endings and beginnings? I wondered now that Eric was leaving.

"SSSS-So, what are you thinking?" he asked.

"About endings and beginnings," I said.

"And?"

"It's just been a really wild year. Relationships, I mean. Like half the time I'm not even sure what's going on."

"M-Maybe you d-don't have to figure it all out. Maybe you sss-shouldn't even try. Just let things b-be; see what happens."

I figured he was talking about us right then. I knew he'd be dating other girls down in Texas, and I'd be seeing other guys back here. It just felt as though there was a huge question mark hanging over my head. But maybe he was right: I tried to control things too much.

"Okay," I said suddenly. "New resolution: Live

one day at a time. Just go with the flow and don't try to guess what will happen next."

He grabbed me then and gave me a real movie-star kiss, bending me backward under the new shade of a box elder, then lifting me back to a standing position.

"What was *that?*" I gasped.

"Didn't you r-recognize it?" he said. "That was what happened next."

A week later, the phone rang, and at first I thought no one was there.

"Hello?" I kept saying. "Hello?" I thought I heard someone breathing on the end of the line, and for a moment I figured it was an obscene call and was about to hang up.

Then a voice said, "A-Alice?" and I realized it was the first time Eric had ever called me on the phone.

"Eric?" I said.

"Yeah, I just c-called to say g-g-good-bye," he said. "We've g-got a six o'clock flight."

"Oh, Eric!" I said. "I hope things turn out great for you."

"Right n-now all I'm thinking about is g-getting my d-driver's license while I'm down there. And mm-missing you."

"Well, good luck on that and everything else," I told

him. And then, "It's wonderful you could call me."

"Yeah. P-Progress. Will you write?" he asked.

"Sure, if you'll answer."

"Of course I will," he said.

"Okay. I'll look for that first letter."

"I m-might surprise you. I might even c-call."

"Even better," I told him.

That's what I mean about change.

I'd no sooner hung up when the phone rang again. I figured Eric had something else he wanted to tell me. But this time it was Karen. "Did you hear?" she asked.

"Hear what?"

"Patrick and Penny. They broke up!"

I was getting dual images in my brain right then of Patrick on one side, Eric on the other. "Really?" I said. "What about?"

"I'm not sure. Penny told Jill it was mutual—that they just didn't seem to have time for each other. I thought you should be the first to know."

"Why?"

"Well, you have a shot at him again," she said.

"Karen, I'm not on a safari," I told her.

"Yeah, but he was yours in the first place, Alice," she argued.

"I don't think anyone ever gave me a title to him," I said.

"You're letting a great opportunity slip by," she said, and hung up.

I'll admit, I waited to see if Patrick would call me that night. If he wanted to get back together. But he didn't, and I didn't call him. And though a part of me would have been glad to have him tell me that all the while he was dating Penny, he was really thinking of me and couldn't live without me, another part was liking this freedom to just explore and see what was around the next corner. To concentrate on who *I* was, for a change, without a boyfriend as an appendage. In a way it was nice to be simply "Alice" again, not "Alice and Patrick," or "Alice and Eric." I think I was feeling better about myself than I could ever remember.

Lester was going out for the evening, and Dad had a season ticket to the National Symphony, so I invited Pamela and Elizabeth for the night. When we get together now, it's usually at my place, because what with Elizabeth's grudge against her parents, and Pamela's dad dating again, and her never quite knowing what's going on between her folks, it's just simpler to have the girls here. I'd hoped Gwen could come over, too, so we could plan some more about camp, but she was going somewhere with her sister.

To take, Elizabeth had written down on a sheet of paper. "Toilet paper," she said.

"What?" I said.

"Camps never have enough toilet paper. I'm bringing my own supply. Tampons, too. And a huge jar of Noxzema."

"Sunscreen," said Pamela. "Write that down."

"M&M's, for the middle of the night if I get hungry," I said. "They're also great bribes if we have discipline problems."

"Boys," said Pamela. "Add those to the list. Big and brawny and cute."

I was just about to get out a frozen pizza when the phone rang. Who could be calling at ten o'clock at night? I wondered. Patrick? I went out in the hall and picked up the phone outside my room.

"Al," came Lester's voice. "Dad there?"

"No. He's at the symphony, remember?"

Lester muttered something I couldn't understand. Then he added, "I forgot."

"What's wrong?"

"Listen. Write this down because I only get one call," he told me. I motioned to Liz to bring me her pad and pencil.

"Okay," I said. "I'm ready."

"I'm at the police station in College Park, and as soon as Dad gets home, ask him to come over here and get me out."

"What?" I cried. "What happened?"

"They took me in for breaking and entering, Al, and I don't know if they're going to set bail or what. Just tell Dad to come over here as soon as he can." He gave me the address and phone number and said he had to go.

"Oh, Les. Did you . . . did Lauren . . . ?"

"Let's just say she didn't think it was all that romantic," Lester said, and hung up.

Pamela and Elizabeth were standing in my doorway, staring at me.

"Lester's been arrested!" I gasped. "For breaking and entering his girlfriend's apartment, and it's all my fault!" I told them about the breakup and what I'd suggested.

"Alice, we've got to get him out!" said Elizabeth. "Your dad may not be home for another hour or two, and Les could be beaten up by then! He could be locked up with murderers and stranglers and . . ."

I was already scared enough, and didn't need that, but Pamela was all fired up, too. "Let's pool our money and take a cab!" she said. "We'll all be character witnesses for Lester, and he'll be indebted to us for life."

I did feel responsible, and I wanted to get him out before Dad got home. So Pamela called a cab, I left a note on the kitchen table for Dad in case he got home before we did, saying I'd be back soon, and when the cab pulled up, all three of us crowded in the backseat and asked the driver to take us to the College Park police station.

We could see him studying us in his rearview mirror. "Any . . . uh . . . particular reason you girls are going to the police station?" he asked.

"A mission of mercy," said Elizabeth, and off we went.

"My gosh, can you *believe* this?" Pamela kept whispering as the cab sped along the beltway toward College Park. "Did you ever think that *we'd* be rescuing *Lester?*"

"He's going to be so glad to see us!" exclaimed Elizabeth.

When the driver pulled up outside police headquarters, he asked, "You want me to wait outside?"

I thought a minute. "Yes, I guess you'd better. I'll come out and let you know."

"Okay, but you're up to eleven dollars now," he said.

I swallowed, and we went inside. A sergeant sat at a desk and was talking with two other officers standing near the back. They all three stopped talking when they saw us.

"Can I help you?" the man at the desk said.

"Yes. I'd like to see my brother, Lester McKinley," I told him.

"Al?" came Lester's voice from somewhere down the hall.

"Lester?" I called back.

And suddenly Elizabeth cried, "Please let him go! We've known him all his life, practically, and he wouldn't hurt anyone, and—"

"Couldn't you just release him to our custody and we'll promise to bring him back for the trial?" Pamela put in.

"Al!" yelled Lester again, and I wondered if inmates were beating him up already.

"Don't let anyone hurt him!" I pleaded. "Just put him in solitary confinement if you won't let him out."

"Uh . . . sister . . . your brother's just getting his things together. The lady refuses to press charges. He's free to go," the sergeant told me.

"What?" I said.

Just then Lester came down the hall, and all three of us rushed over and threw our arms around him. I was crying because this all had happened on account of me.

Lester shook us loose and fumbled around in his pocket for his car keys. "Damnation!" he said. "My car's back at her apartment." He turned to the officers. "Now that you got me out here, how about a ride back?"

"Sorry, buddy. The lady called 911, and we responded. We were just doing our job. One-way transportation only."

"It's okay, Lester, I've got a cab waiting," I told him.

He stared at me. "What?"

"It's all arranged," I said. "The cab will drive you back to get your car, and we'll go with you."

We went outside and the three of us crawled in the taxi again while Lester got in front with the driver. The cabbie looked at him warily, and Lester gave him Lauren's address.

"It's okay," I told the driver. "He's not violent or anything."

"Al!" said Lester.

"Only when he's being studly," Elizabeth said, giggling.

"And then he's wild! Pure animal energy!" purred Pamela.

Les turned around. "Will you *stop?*"

We all got out at Lauren's apartment building, paid the cab driver, and climbed in Lester's car. The windows in the ground-floor apartment were dark. I figured she had probably turned out the lights and was watching from a window.

Lester didn't even glance toward the building. He pulled away from the curb with a screech of tires, and headed back toward Silver Spring.

"Who wants to be dropped off first?" he asked.

"No such luck, Les. They're spending the night," I said.

He groaned. "Listen," he said. "I would really appreciate it if you guys wouldn't tell Dad any of this."

"Okay, but you have to tell us what really happened, then," I said, eager to bargain.

"Oh, good grief!" Lester said. He was quiet for a minute or two, but finally said, "Lauren had asked me days ago to return her house key, so . . . I was returning the key. I just happened to let myself in first, and was sitting at her kitchen table waiting for her when she walked in. With a new boyfriend, it so happens, a professor in the physics department. I was only going to plead my case, but she never gave me the chance. She pretended I was a student obsessed with her, and called 911 to make it convincing."

"Maybe you should have brought flowers," I said.

"It wouldn't have helped," Les said bitterly. "She obviously hadn't told her new boyfriend about me, and especially didn't want him to know she'd given me her key. That really teed me off, so I was standing there shouting at her when the police arrived. . . . All this time she's just been using me to get acquainted, find her way around. . . ."

"Oh, poor Les," said Pamela. "There are other fish in the ocean, you know."

"It's always darkest before the light," said Elizabeth.

"It may seem awful now, Lester, but tonight's the first night of the rest of your life," I told him.

"Are they offering a course now in platitudes at your school? *Bartlett's Quotations?*" Lester said. "Just forget it, will you? It's over. I'm lucky to have found out now. But remember, not a word to Dad. I don't want to worry him. He's too happy these days."

I agreed.

Dad was already home when we got there, standing in the kitchen, puzzling over my note.

"Well!" he said, as we all trooped in. "Where have you been?"

"Out with Lester for a night on the town," I said.

"Oh?" Dad looked pleased. Pleased, I guess, that Lester was getting over his breakup so soon.

"A little reality contact, that's all," Lester said.

"I'm glad to hear it," Dad told him. "I had a great evening, too. All Schubert and Mendelssohn. A real treat."

"Then everybody's happy!" I said, and led the girls back up to my room. Les had paid the cab fare for us, so we weren't out anything.

We lay on my bed a long time discussing the evening—Lester's breakup and all.

"You know what that means, don't you?" said Elizabeth.

"What *what* means?"

"His having the key to her apartment," said Elizabeth. "It means they were having sex. When you give a man a key to your apartment, it's his invitation. You know . . . the guy is the key, and the woman's the keyhole, and—"

"You *were* dropped on your head as a baby," I said. "Maybe she let him have a key so he could study there, where it was quiet. How do you know?"

"Yeah, and maybe they just liked to get together and play Tiddly Winks," said Pamela. "Anyone who believes they were just friends, please raise your hand."

"Okay, maybe. But this keyhole business—"

"It is, it is! Everything's symbolic!" said Elizabeth, warming to the subject. "Pistons and cylinders, candles and holders—"

"Plugs and sockets," said Pamela.

There was a tap on the door, and Lester opened it a crack. "Everyone decent?" he called.

"No, Les, we're all lying here naked," Pamela called. "Come on in and join the party."

We giggled.

Les opened the door tentatively, and finally all the way.

"See?" said Pamela. "That didn't stop him one bit."

"Just wanted to say thanks, Al," Lester said. "It was a comedy of errors from the get-go. At least she had enough decency not to press charges, but I'm still steamed."

"Well, don't do anything rash, Lester," I said.

"Don't worry. I'm off women for the duration."

"The duration of what?" I asked. "The next three years at the U? Till you get your Ph.D.? What?"

"I didn't say I'm a eunuch, Al. The duration of the summer, anyway."

He said good night and went back to his room.

"You know what that means . . ." said Elizabeth.

"What *what* means?" I said.

"That he's not going to be a eunuch. A eunuch can't have intercourse, you know, so if Lester's *not* going to be a eunuch, then it can only mean that—"

"Good night, Elizabeth," I said. "Sweet dreams." And I turned out the light.

15

Sylvia

Dad was in a cleaning frenzy. I thought we had already done spring cleaning, but he said we'd hardly begun. Sylvia was coming exactly two days before I left for my three weeks as an assistant camp counselor, and Dad wanted the house to be perfect. When a house has been as imperfect as ours has been for all the years we've lived here, it's sort of a lost cause, I think. Lester and I considered moving to the Y for the week, but we wanted to do what we could to make Sylvia feel welcome. So I finally called Aunt Sally in Chicago.

"Alice, sweetheart, it's been so long since I've heard your voice!" she said. "How *are* you?"

For a moment I was tempted to tell her that Lester had been in jail, because I knew she would catch the next plane to Maryland if I did, and then, as long as she was here, she would clean the house from top to bottom and save us the trouble.

Not only clean the house, but bake a couple of pies while she was at it.

"Is anything wrong, Alice?" Aunt Sally said, and sounded worried.

"Not at all, we're just fine!" I said. "Except that Miss Summers is due back from England in a week, and Dad wants the house to be perfect. I don't know where to begin."

There was a long moment of silence, and I was afraid I'd already said too much—that Aunt Sally was even then looking up the number for United Airlines in the yellow pages. But finally she said, "If there are still any clothes of your mother's around, Alice, don't let her wear them."

"What?" I said, wondering how we got from cleaning to clothes.

"Out of respect for Marie," she said.

"Aunt Sally, I really don't think Sylvia wants Mom's clothes. Trust me," I said.

"I mean, how would you feel if you were dead and your husband brought home a new wife?" Aunt Sally continued.

Sometimes it's best to not even try to answer.

"Well," she said, "as far as housecleaning, Sylvia's not moving in right away, is she? When is the wedding?"

"July twenty-eighth," I said.

"Then I'd let her worry about the cleaning.

She'll have two whole months to clean the house herself. Unless, of course, she's moving in *before* they're married, which I trust is not the case, not with you and Lester there."

I had to smile. "No, I don't think so, Aunt Sally. She has a house of her own, you know."

"Good. Then here's all you have to remember, Alice. *Susie Dances Very Well.*"

"Huh?" I said.

"That's what my mother taught me: SDVW— **S**usie **D**ances **V**ery **W**ell. S stands for 'scrub sinks, tub, and floor'; D stands for 'dust all flat surfaces'; V stands for 'vacuum carpets and rugs'; and W stands for 'wash windows, towels, and bedding.' If you can remember that, the house will be clean enough when Sylvia gets there, and you don't have to worry about doing anything more."

"Thanks, Aunt Sally," I said uncertainly.

"And Alice, if she *does* move in before they're married, tell her I disapprove."

Dad didn't pay the least bit of attention to *Susie Dances Very Well*. You would think our house had termites, vermin, bats' nests, and mold, the way he got us up early Sunday morning and made us attack the windows, the woodwork, the floors, and rugs. Every finger mark disappeared from the walls, every smudge on a window, every spot on a rug.

Lester rented a rug cleaner from the supermart, and we vacuumed and laundered; we dusted and scrubbed. We stripped the beds and washed the blankets, aired the pillows and cleaned the closets.

By seven that evening, Dad was asleep on the couch, Lester lay sprawled on his back on the living room rug, and I was curled up in my beanbag chair, too tired to move.

I guess none of us heard the doorbell. Dad was snoring, Les was snoring, even *I* was snoring, probably, when I was vaguely conscious of the doorbell, then footsteps, then Marilyn standing over me, saying, "Alice? Alice? Is everything all right here?"

Dad stirred, Les raised his head and plunked it down again, and I heard Marilyn say, "Thank goodness! When no one answered the door, I looked through the window and thought you were all overcome by carbon monoxide or something." Then she saw the buckets and brooms and mops. "Wow!" she said. *"House Beautiful!"*

"I'd get up and ask you to sit down, Marilyn, but I don't think I can move," said Dad.

"I won't even try," murmured Lester.

I just sat up and rubbed my eyes.

"I brought over the inventory you asked for, Mr. M. I worked up some figures at home," Marilyn said. "I thought you might want them."

"Just put them there on the table, will you?" said Dad, his lips barely moving.

Marilyn looked around at us. "Have you eaten?"

"Too tired to cook," said Dad.

And suddenly Marilyn became Mother Superior. She went to the phone and ordered antipasti and veal scallopini to be delivered, with an order of cannoli for dessert. Then she set the table, lit some candles, and when the food was delivered, paid for it herself, which finally brought Dad to his feet so he could reimburse her.

By then, the smell of the food had revived us, we managed to get ourselves to the table, and invited Marilyn to eat with us.

"Well done, Marilyn," Dad said. "Hiring you was one of the best things I ever did."

"Now's your chance, Mar," Lester joked. "Ask for a raise." We all laughed.

"As a matter of fact," Dad went on, "she got a raise just last week, and she's worth every penny of it."

Marilyn beamed.

I watched Les watching Marilyn, and Marilyn watching Dad, and Dad eating his scallopini, and thought what a great, happy family we'd be if Les would just marry Marilyn in a double-ring ceremony with Dad and Sylvia. We could all live here together, and . . .

"I can't stay any longer," Marilyn said, before she

had dessert. "Jack's coming over a little later, and I want to be there."

"Big date, huh?" Les said.

"Yes. He's pretty special," Marilyn said, and smiled. "Well, thanks for letting me stay, Mr. M. Glad you enjoyed the dinner. Double glad you weren't all dead! Scared me to death for a minute there."

And then she was gone.

It could have been so perfect—Les could have fallen in love with Marilyn again, and proposed over the cannoli. He could have forgotten all about Lauren and being in jail and . . . Life isn't like that, I guess. Sometimes change *isn't* for the better.

I was afraid he'd really be depressed now. Not only had Lauren dumped him, but his old reliable girlfriend was seeing someone new. Lester, though, looked refreshed and relieved. Maybe he was feeling the same way I was now: free to enjoy being unattached for a while.

"Thank you, you two," Dad said to us later as he walked through the living room, the clean scent of Lemon Pledge and Windex wafting through the house. "Sylvia's going to be impressed."

"I think Sylvia will have eyes only for you, Dad, and all this work won't matter," Les told him.

We decided that we'd all go to the airport to meet her. We wanted to welcome her back as a family, so she would feel really glad about moving into our house and taking Mom's place. Les and I wanted to show that we loved her, too.

So the three of us stood at the gate at Dulles when her flight was due, knowing she'd be coming through customs, that she'd be tired from the long flight, but we were ready to give her and Dad space once we got home. Les, in fact, was going to take me to the movies.

All these months, Dad had been the patient one, the calm one, the man who could put his dreams on hold till his love was in his arms again. And now, waiting for Sylvia, he was as jumpy as I'd ever seen him, like a horse at the starting gate. He'd be talking with Lester and me one minute, then striding over to the window to see if a shuttle was coming yet from the far terminal. And as each shuttle arrived and disgorged its passengers, he watched every face, hoping for a first glimpse of her. Checking his watch, raising himself up on his toes to see over the crowd, crossing his arms, then uncrossing them again.

And then, coming out of a fourth shuttle, there she was—the light brown hair, the beautifully shaped brows, the wispy green silk scarf on top of her blouse, her smile. She was as beautiful as ever, but more tired looking than I'd ever seen her. Her eyes, of course, were on Dad, but they lit up, too, when they saw Les and me, and she put down her carry-on bag and opened her arms to embrace us all at once.

But Dad got to her first and couldn't help himself. He lifted her a few inches off the floor and spun around with her as though he were twenty years old, and what happened next came so fast, we could hardly believe it: Sylvia suddenly pushed away from him, stepped backward, and threw up on the floor. On Dad's shoes, in fact, splattering the cuffs of his pants as well.

"Darling!" cried Dad.

She only gagged again and vomited a second time. People around us averted their eyes and gave us a wide berth as they passed, and an airline employee phoned for a janitor.

"Oh, I'm so sorry, Ben!" Sylvia said, wiping her mouth, the front of her blouse stained.

"Sweetheart, you're sick!" Dad cried, putting an arm around her.

"Just air sick. There was such turbulence, and . . ." She clamped her mouth shut, afraid she would vomit again, but I was already heading for a rest room behind us to get some wet paper towels.

I was back almost immediately, and Dad took them from me. Gently, lovingly, he wiped her face, a spot on her scarf, her blouse, and only when she had been escorted to a chair did he tend to his own pants and shoes. A man with a mop and pail was coming down the corridor, and we moved away to sit with Sylvia.

"How embarrassing!" she said, smiling at us wanly.

"For a grand entrance, Sylvia, I'd say you win the prize," Les joked, and she laughed.

So it happens to the best and the beautiful, too, I was thinking. All the embarrassing, ridiculous, gross, humiliating things that had happened to me in my fifteen years happened to other people as well, even grown-up career women who were madly in love. It was comforting in a way to know that I wasn't alone, but terrifying to think that these things go on forever. The only thing that changes, I guess, is the way we react to them.

"We're not going out to the car until you're feeling better," Dad said, leaning over her and kissing her forehead.

"Hard to believe, but I'm feeling *much* better, now that I'm off the plane," Sylvia said. "I guess the only thing that would have been worse is if I'd been sick on my seatmates." She turned to Lester and me. "Well, you *know* how I am. How are *you?*"

"Glad to see you, that's what," I said. "I can't believe you're here to stay."

"Neither can I," said Sylvia, smiling at Dad. For a long minute their eyes feasted on each other, like their eyes were doing all the talking. And finally, when the color had returned to Sylvia's face and she seemed herself again, she said, "Let's go home."

Les and I stayed at the house for only a half hour or so, and then we headed for the movies. We got there twenty minutes early, but felt we should give Dad and Sylvia as much time alone as we could. So we ate most of our popcorn ahead of time and drank half our drinks as well.

"That's what I want." I sighed, thinking of Dad and Sylvia again. "Did you see the gentle way he wiped her face, Lester? I'll bet some men would have been disgusted at a woman throwing up in public, especially all over his shoes. But it was as though Dad didn't even notice. All he cared about was her. When I think about marrying, I'm going to look for someone like that."

"So what are you going to do? Give each potential husband the barf test?" he asked. "Puke on his shoes and see what happens?"

"No, just pay attention to how he treats me when I'm sick. Like, when we can't go somewhere we'd planned because I'm having cramps or have a bad cold. Or when I'm feeling really upset and depressed, if he can talk to me about it, or whether he just wants me to get over it."

I was thinking of Faith and Ron right then, and

the way Ron never seemed to care what *she* was feeling. The way he got his jollies, it seemed, was by ordering Faith around.

"It works both ways, you know," Les said. "Some girls—and I've known a few—want to be catered to like princesses. Like the guy is her servant, and it's *her* feelings, *her* moods that are important. She never stops to consider what kind of a day *he* might have had, or how little money's in his pocket."

I remembered the time Patrick got on the school bus and threw up in the aisle, how embarrassing it was for him. And how the next day the kids wanted to tease him about it, but I was the only one who wouldn't go along with the joke. I felt pretty good just then to know that I could consider a boy's feelings, and at the same time, I felt a sudden rush of missing Patrick.

"Neither one of us has a love life right now, Les. Do you realize that?" I asked.

He stopped chewing, unsure of what I was going to suggest, I guess. "So?"

"So, are we depressed, or what?"

"I don't know. Are we Siamese twins sharing the same brain?"

"It's just that I'm not always sure *how* I'm feeling. I've had a great year, actually. . . ."

"So go with the great year! Quit thinking about

what you're *supposed* to feel, *supposed* to have, *supposed* to be—just enjoy the moment, Al."

"What about you? What about *your* year?" I asked him.

"I had a great time with Lauren, but now it's over, and *I'm* enjoying the present. That's enough."

I leaned over and gazed dramatically into his eyes. "*Are* you enjoying this moment, Lester— sitting in the theater beside your sister?"

"Get your hand out of the popcorn, Al, and I'll enjoy it a whole lot more," he said.

BE SURE TO READ *ALL* OF
THE ALICE BOOKS

Also check out Alice on the Web at
http://www.simonsayskids.com/alice
  · Read and exchange letters with
    Phyllis Reynolds Naylor!
  · Get the latest news about Alice!
  · Take Alice quizzes!
  · Check out the Alice books
    reading group guide!

"Naylor's funny, poignant coming-of-age series . . .
has continued to serve as a kind of road map for a
girl growing up today." —*Booklist*